KITRA

Gideon Marcus

Journey Press
journeypress.com

Vista, California
Journey Press

Journey Press
P.O. Box 1932
Vista, CA 92085
© Gideon Marcus, 2020

CREDITS
Interior art: Lorelei Esther, 2020
Cover design: DLR Cover Designs

First Printing March 2020

ISBN: 978-1-951320-02-7

Published in the United States of America

journeypress.com

To Janice, the original Kitra

Chapter 1

At 1,000 meters above the ground, my right wing dipped down, and I felt a lurch in my stomach as if I were going over a waterfall. The east edge of the city sprawled out before my right window at an increasing angle. The invisible columns of hot air that were the source of lift for my sailplane had disappeared. My fault. I shouldn't have gotten distracted. There was no time to worry about that now, though. I spiraled in ever widening circles, trying to find my lost lift. I had to do it by feel, sensing for tell-tale little changes in vertical speed, an increase in pressure of the seat against me. But there was nothing; just a sinking feeling as my ears popped, heading downward.

A glance at the altimeter showed I had passed 750 meters. I was running out of options. I could keep hunting for the thermals rising from the hot plains at the edge of the city, but if they weren't there anymore, that would mean a hard landing far from the gliderport. For a moment, I considered just riding all the way down anyway and activating the emergency antigravity brake, a tiny battery powered thing that would slow my descent in the last seconds before landing. I grimaced at the thought. I'd never had to use it before, and it would be an embarrassment, an admission of failure. Not to mention a long walk home.

I squinted at the distant towers of Denizli. That was an option. It was about 39 o' clock, and the sun had warmed the downtown streets and plazas for twenty hours. They might provide enough lift. Then again, they might not. It was nearly sunset. Anyway, flying at low altitude over the capital was a sure way to run into the air traffic cops.

1

I continued my spiral, flaps fully off, trying to maximize my glideslope to get somewhere, anywhere there might be lift. I was already down to 500 meters. I looked around for a ridge or hill. Maybe I could use the wind that blows upward when a horizontal breeze hits a slope? No, no luck. All the good ones were too far away.

Bright light filled the cockpit, dazzling me for a moment. The glancing rays of the setting sun reflected off the ocean, shimmering all the way to the limits of vision. I hadn't realized I was so close to the shore. Shielding my eyes from the glare, I grinned. Of course! I knew where to find a ridge after all. An invisible one.

I waited until the plane was facing the shore and then straightened out, making a beeline for the ocean. Would I have enough time? I looked down and swallowed. Suburban houses, stores, a school, were drifting uncomfortably closer and closer beneath me. Then, at 150 meters, buildings gave way to a sprawling stretch of beach. It curved away on both sides for kilometers, to skyscrapers toward the city, to preserved parkland in the other direction. I headed toward the greenery, aiming for the source of lift I knew existed parallel to the shore.

The altimeter read 100 meters as I sailed over the crashing breakers. The glider jerked in the chaotic air flow, and I gripped the controls tightly to keep it steady. My back pressed into the seat as the plane's wings caught the winds that zoomed up where the warm air of the land met the colder air above the sea. The plane jittered, then smoothed out, climbing faster and faster. In no time, I was at 300 meters and still rising, wisps of marine layer clouds breaking across the glider's wingtips as I soared above them. The greenish sky of Vatan was turning gold in the sunset, and the planet's rings formed an arch that started at the horizon and vaulted high overhead. I breathed a sigh of relief and punched a fist against my knee in victory.

At 2000 meters, more than high enough to make it back to the gliderport, I eased the plane into a smooth bank, aiming for the traffic pattern that would eventually get me home. Then I gave my forehead a little rap for my lapse of concentration. Soaring is something you can do for hours on end, and it's easy to slide into a sort of trance, letting your hands guide the glider on their own while your mind wanders. That's when you get into trouble.

I settled into my seat, blowing out a breath. But even with that object lesson, now that the danger had passed, my thoughts went right back to what had distracted me in the first place. The decision I'd been so sure of last night.

Once again, I got those butterflies in my stomach that had nothing to do with flying, at least not directly. Was this really going to be my final flight? Was I really going to sell my glider? I loved soaring, and I loved my little plane. It had given me good service for two years. Flying in it had become almost as familiar, as easy as walking. Did I really want to give it up? Could I?

I looked out the right window, watching the setting sun ignite the ocean horizon with green flame. It was a sight I never got tired of.

I bit my lip. It wouldn't just be the glider. It'd be selling virtually everything I owned, just to start the next phase of my plan. Ridding myself of a lifetime of security. It would be safer to just pick out a college, plan a career. If I wanted to follow in my late mother's footsteps, I could get a degree in interstellar studies and join the state department. In fifteen years, maybe only ten, I'd be eligible for a diplomatic mission off-planet. It was what my uncle, my mother's brother, wanted me to do. It was the safe route.

I shook my head. No. That wasn't the course for me. It was too long, and the pay-off might never happen. I needed to stick to the plan.

Next week, Marta and I would go to the auction yards where they sold second-hand and decommissioned spaceships. In my bank account would be my inheritance plus the proceeds of the sale of nearly all of my possessions, including the glider. It should be enough to buy a ship of my very own. Once I assembled a crew, I wouldn't be Kitra Yilmaz anymore. I'd be *Captain* Kitra Yilmaz.

That thought dispelled the last of my doubts. I smiled and gave the control panel a fond pat, a goodbye embrace. Then I steered for home.

From now on, the soaring I'd do would be among the stars.

Fifteenth of Red, 306 P.S.V. (Launch -53 (Standard))

Marta stood out from the drabness of the auction yard, like a lone flower in a bare field. She wore bright colors and flowing skirts — completely impractical for this dusty, dirty place. Maybe she'd expected something more glamorous.

"You didn't have to come with me," I ventured.

Marta shook her head, brown curls bobbing, and flashed me a cute, dimpled smile. "Don't be silly. I'm going to be on the ship, too. I wanted to come."

I smiled, relieved. "I'm glad you did. There's no way I could do this alone."

She gave my shoulder a reassuring squeeze. "You'll do fine."

The yard was a dingy flat piece of land out on the north end of the capital. I'd been there before, with my parents a few times, and then, recently, several times by myself. It wasn't a pretty place, peppered as it was with random junk: pieces of old hulls that had fallen off and rusted where they lay, and lot marker beacons that blinked endlessly, powered by the wireless grid. There was always litter and garbage strewn about. A wide highway went right up to the edge of the field. That was so the antigrav tugs could bring the ships to be sold; generally, the vessels to be auctioned couldn't make it here on their own power. It was a place that hardly anyone could find beautiful.

Still, every month, there was a crowd of people. The same types, if not all the same faces. I nodded greetings to a few of them I'd come to know, people like me nursing dreams of getting a cheap ship of their own. There were also the ones walking around in suits and making calls on their little *sayars*. They worked for small-time shipping or salvage companies. Off to one side, I saw a familiar couple, ship hobbyists with palm-sized technician's *sayars* like mine, who came every month to tap out notes and take holos of the ships. Most of the attendees, though, were there for the excitement, just to see how much a person would spend on a rusting hulk.

At 13:45, just as the mid-morning sun broke through the clouds, the auctioneer arrived. He was wearing a purple suit and hovering on an antigravity disk.

"Hello, everyone," he said in a pleasant, practiced tone. "The auction for the month of Red is beginning. Let's bring out Salvage #1."

I rubbed the fingers of my right hand together in anticipation. There were always a half-dozen or more ships on sale every month. Vatan was an important world with a naval yard. It wasn't quite at the edge of the Empire anymore, but it had been for a long time. A lot of trade lanes ran through the Yeni Izmir system, Vatan being its most important planet, so there were lots of ships around. And while ships were built to last a long time, they did eventually wear out. When they got too broken down to resell, or if an owner was just in a hurry to unload, or if the state seized a ship in lieu of missed taxes, it ended up here.

Salvage #1 was a squat, ugly thing so big that it took two tractors and four antigravity holders to carry. It was way too large for my purposes, some kind of bulk freighter. And it was only part of one; once it was brought in front of the audience, I could see that most of the back half had been sheared off. The open cargo bay looked like a giant cavern. There was no explanation as to how it got this way. Maybe a meteor had hit it. No one bid on the hulk, and it was dragged off to the holding section of the lot where the salvage companies could pick over the corpse of the ship like vultures, making offers on its pieces.

The next two salvages were brought in as a pair. They were Package Boats, small ships whose barrel shape was familiar to everyone in the Empire, and utterly useless to me. They hadn't had engines even before they got here. Just room enough for a Jump Drive, a hundred tons of cargo, and a poor cramped mail courier who spent a week traveling between stars and then couldn't even get to their destination under their own power. They had to be picked up by a local tug. I watched as the pair was snagged by a second-rate Frontier postal company.

My breath caught as they towed in Salvage #4. It was beautiful, a slender green thing that flashed in the sun. It looked well-maintained, too. Not exactly what I was looking for, at only a hundred tons and not much room for cargo, but it probably flew like a dream. I looked at Marta hopefully and reached for my *sayar*, prepared to make an offer. The bidding started at 400,000 credits. I quickly put my *sayar* back. There was no way. Oh well. A yacht wasn't what I was after, and I was sure the fellow who bought it would be very happy.

I was starting to get worried. There couldn't be too many ships left, and nothing had been remotely close to usable. My spirits sank even further when Salvage #5 came out. Its type wasn't even recognizable under the grime and the mold. It smelled bad, too. Another one for the junkers.

Five for five. Was I going to have to come back next month? I couldn't really afford the delay. Summer vacation was only so long, and while *I* didn't have school at the end of it, the rest of my intended crew did.

The voice of the auctioneer boomed over the flat, ship-littered field. "Last auction of the day." I swallowed. An orange tractor towed the sixth ship out to us, floating on a pair of antigrav units.

It wasn't pretty. It was about the size of a big airliner, covered bow to stern with a hard gray preserving foam. It had wings, sort of, like a plucked chicken has wings. There were huge gaps in its triangular shape, unsettling, like empty eye sockets. A gust of wind blew around the ship as it came to a halt, and I wiped grit from my eyes, trying to figure out what kind of vessel it was, or more accurately, had been.

"Salvage #6," the announcer said. "*Yarsihar* Class Scout, Imperial Navy. Two Hundred Tons. Hull Only."

That explained the ship's condition. Like all of the ex-military vessels that made it to auction, everything of value that could be stripped out had been: weapons, navigation controls, the fusion power plant, the engines, the Drive. To an unseasoned eye, it looked pretty bad.

It looked bad to me, too. The *Yarsihars* were old. I'd certainly never seen one in the wild, and this one looked like it had been run to the ground. It must have been one of the last to retire. I pulled out my *sayar* and called up holos of *Yarsihars* in service. Fleshed out, they looked pretty good, actually, but the images of graceful ships didn't much resemble the old thing in front of me. Well, I knew my ship was probably going to be a fixer-upper...

"100,000 is the opening bid," came the announcer's voice. My eyebrows went up, and I glanced over at Marta again. She looked a question at me, and I nodded just a touch. I'd budgeted 150,000 credits for the ship. This was well within my range, provided no one drove the price up too high.

A few seconds stretched out before a bored-looking guy in a business cloak called out, his voice amplified: "100,000."

I bit my lip. Was it worth fighting for? I didn't want to buy the thing just out of desperation. On the other hand, it was the right size, and Navy ships were built to last. I looked hard at it again, fleshing the duralloy bones in my mind, imagining it with a shiny new skin. Yes. I saw what it could be. I decided to go for it.

"105,000," I replied, waving my hand awkwardly. There were giggles from some of the people in the audience, and I thrust my hand back in my pocket.

The announcer's voice again: "I hear 105,000. Do I hear 110?"

There was a pause, and I got hopeful. Everyone else was looking at business cloak. He was the only one besides me who was interested.

"110," he said briskly.

I blurted without thinking. "115!" The other guy's expression didn't change, but I saw a muscle twitch in his forehead. I'd surprised him with the speed of my reply.

After a pause, he said, "120." His voice was calm.

"125!" I called.

Another pause. Then, "130."

I had the feeling he was wavering, so I pressed the attack. "140!" My voice cracked.

A little smile grew under his thin mustache. He looked at me for the first time, cold dark eyes in a fleshy face. "One hundred and fifty-five." He enunciated his words slowly and precisely. *Run along and play, little girl,* they seemed to say. His smug face annoyed me so much that I completely forgot my budget, matched his smirk with one of my own, and declared, "175!" It was all I could do not to stamp my foot, too.

Marta grabbed my hand as my amplified voice echoed around the yard. The crowd was looking at me now. One of them licked her lips expectantly. There was silence. *That* had set the jerk back on his heels.

"I hear 175," the barker said. "175. 175 going once..."

My mouth was dry. I looked at my opponent, my eyes wide and daring. It was a brave front—he couldn't see my heart thudding.

"175 going twice..."

Business cloak looked down and scuffed the ground with his boot.

"Sold to attendee 38! Please come and inspect your prize."

I let out a puff of air. Marta tugged at my fingers, and I looked up at her. She wasn't smiling. "Kitra, that's most of your money, isn't it?" she asked.

I nodded, wondering just where my stupid mouth had gotten me. The purple-suited auctioneer came down from his floater and waved for me to follow him. I walked toward the ship, not feeling my feet. I'd done it, but what had I done? The gleaming scout I'd conjured in my mind's eye disappeared. Salvage #6 was just an ugly, holed hulk again. My heart sank.

The announcer, a thin man whose pale skin was made more pronounced by his loud suit, was standing by the ship when I got there. He pointed his *sayar* at the ship's hatch. The door slid into the hull obligingly. At least *that* worked. I followed him inside, Marta still clutching my hand. She wrinkled her nose at the smell, a sharp tang of ozone, plastic, and dust.

"May I?" I asked. Purple-suit waved me in. I took out my *sayar* and turned it into a torch, illuminating the lower corridor. I tried to remember the *Yarsihar* layout. There were stairs, which I knew led up to the common areas and the bridge. Ahead was the service corridor, at the end of which was the engine's socket. A good enough place to start.

My footsteps rang hollowly on the unfoamed floor, leaving dusty footprints. It must have been abandoned for years. I stopped at the aft end of the ship where there once had been a powerful thruster, driven by the same force that made the sun shine. Now, there was just a cavernous gap ringed with frayed wires and sheared piping.

Sure enough, it was just a skeleton. Lord. 175,000 credits! What had I been thinking?

I sighed, playing the torch on the ceiling with a half-hearted gesture. But instead of illuminating an empty, corroded hyperdrive mount, the light shone back in my eyes, diffracted into a million brilliant rainbows by a textured porcelain surface. My eyes widened, and my heart pulsed in my ears as I realized what I'd found.

"Oh my," I heard the auctioneer say. "I'm surprised they left that in."

I looked at Marta, a wild grin on my face.

Chapter 2

Seventeenth of Red, 306 P.S.V. (Launch -51 (Standard))

"There's a Jump Drive!" I said, loud enough that the customers at the next table over looked at me for a moment before turning back to their coffee and conversations.

Across the table, Fareedh leaned back in his seat, a converted spaceliner couch. His dark eyes took on a faraway expression. I crossed my fingers mentally and hoped this would be the thing that got him on board. Fareedh was the newest member of our friend group. We'd only met him last year. But he was essential for my plans.

Fareedh focused on me and drummed his fingers on the low table once, twice. The music and chatter in *Le Frontière* seemed unusually loud while I waited for him to answer. At last, he said in his gentle low voice, "That speeds up your plans, doesn't it, Kitra?"

Your plans. Damn. I really wanted Fareedh in the crew, maybe not just for his programming skills. He was strikingly good-looking, though he looked like he might blow over in a stiff Vatan wind. Older than me, with black wavy hair and dark skin about my color.

"You're not interested?" I asked.

He shrugged. "I don't suppose they left a ship's *sayar* in there too, did they?"

I shook my head, my ponytail tickling my neck. "Nothing I'd feel comfortable using. You'd have to put in a new system from scratch and program it yourself." I smiled challengingly, hoping to pique his pride. "If you're up for it, that is."

Fareedh's eyes flashed, widening slightly for just a moment. It was very appealing. "Oh, I'm up for anything," he purred.

I could feel my cheeks flushing. I turned away, getting a little angry. He wasn't taking this seriously. Marta and Peter came through the door then, easy to spot since both were just shy of two meters. I felt relieved to have the back-up. I waved at them, and they waved back. They navigated the crowded tables of *Le Frontière*, weaving their way toward ours. The coffee house was packed, mostly with students from the nearby university. It was music night, when local acts performed. The pair playing in the center of the shop were some of the best Erkki had gotten: a flautist with a powderpuff afro, who trilled a clever and complex melody while her partner, a boy with long, dark hair, played a complementary part on the guitar. Above them, space-themed holos slowly faded in and out. At the moment, it was the yellow globe of Talvi, an old Frontier colony about 12 parsecs away.

Our friends eventually reached us, and Marta squeezed her plump form onto the bench seat next to Peter, automatically reaching up to smooth down his perpetually messy blond hair. I flinched a little, inwardly, remembering how I used to hate it when she'd do that to me in public. Peter, on the other hand, relaxed and leaned into her touch. Yeah, they definitely made a better couple than we had.

"Heya, hero," Peter said, grinning at me, blue eyes twinkling.

"Heya, mouse," I countered automatically. Not that the nickname fit anymore. He was built like a professional wrestler, now. He hadn't been bullied in years.

"Did you see my latest contribution?" He pointed to one of the display cases on the far wall, past the musicians. The thing inside was pretty big.

"I have no idea what that is," I said, smiling. "It looks like an electric snail."

"Not quite," he said. "It's an old regulator from a chemical thruster. It's an exact replica. I built it a while ago, figured it was time to put it to good use."

I had a flash of memory: Peter hunched over a bigger-than-usual pile of junk, his pale, angular features focused in concentration. He hadn't come out of there for days, not even for his daily work-out routine. His sister had brought him sandwiches every day, and probably a portable toilet.

"What'd Erkki give you for it?" Fareedh asked.

"20% off for the next year."

He looked mildly impressed. "Not bad."

"All right," Peter said, turning to me again. "So what's the news on this latest adventure you've dragged us all into?"

"Did she tell you?" Marta asked Fareedh.

Fareedh nodded. "She told me." His tone suggested a maddening lack of interest.

It was time to lay down my trump card. "Not everything," I said.

That got all eyes on me. If this didn't convince Fareedh, I didn't know what would. I cleared my throat. "So, first off, thank you for being on board." I directed that at Marta and Peter. "It's a lot of work, and there's no way it could get done without you. Now here's the good news."

I leaned forward in my chair. "Our plans have gotten a bit of a boost," I said, smiling at Peter. "It turns out that the ship I got wasn't completely stripped. That's the secret Marta's been keeping." I locked eyes with Fareedh, "I told you the ship's got a Drive, but that's not the end of it. It's a Type Three." I paused for effect. "One Jump. Ten light years."

He just gave me a polite smile. Did nothing impress him?

"The ship has a Drive?" Peter asked, an odd note in his voice.

"Yes!" I glanced at him, looking forward to the excitement I was sure he'd show. "The Navy just left it in, like they'd forgotten about it."

"Oh." His voice was flat.

My smile froze.

"This is going to be great!" Marta said cheerfully. "I don't remember if I told you. My professor's giving me extension credit for my project. If the bio-scrubber keeps the ship's air fresh, I get an A."

"Which is the most important aspect," Fareedh said, deadpan.

"Well yeah...and keeping us alive," Marta admitted. "Which it definitely will for at least three weeks. I guarantee it," she added brightly.

"Three weeks is a pretty tight margin, isn't it?" Peter asked.

"It'll be fine," she said. "A week in Jump out, a week back. That leaves a week to fly around." She put her elbows on the table, fingers interlocked. "It's not like we're going to be plunging into the unknown. We'll stick to settled planets until I improve my system, is all."

Peter looked at Marta. "And," he began uncertainly, "that's with a crew of five?"

Marta nodded. "Yes, of course."

"So it'd last longer with fewer people," he said.

"Sure, but..." She frowned. "Why would we have fewer people?"

"I'm just not sold on the idea, that's all." He folded his big arms.

I blinked. "Wait, what? You were all for the idea last week."

"Sure. When we were talking about doing a couple of in-system runs out to Four and back."

I couldn't understand his attitude. "So isn't this better? With a Type Three, we could go *anywhere*. We could fly to the Core Worlds and back in less than a year if we want."

Peter shook his head. "That's what I'm saying. Look, Kitra. I know this has been your dream for a long time, and I said I'd help. But I've got two more years of school to finish, and classes resume in three months. I didn't sign up for a hyperspace jaunt. How can I afford the time?"

Again, *my* dream. Was I the only one excited about having a ship, one that came with a built-in ticket to the stars? I looked at Peter, stung, then shifted my focus to the ceiling holo, now of a gas giant's swirling belts, and slowly counted to five in my head.

It didn't help, so I stood up. "I'm going to put in our orders," I said. Maybe it would be easier when all of us were here. I was sure Pinky would back me up.

"Can we get sugar this time?" Fareedh asked, a slight smile on his lips.

I tried to smile back at him. "Philistine," I said.

Marta shrugged. "He's got a point..."

"I'll see what I can do."

Things weren't going well at all. I had that sick feeling in my stomach, like someone had turned the antigravity off. I needed a few minutes to regroup. I turned and headed for the little counter where Erkki stood, taking and making the orders. He might know how to fix things.

I caught Erkki just as he'd finished with a customer. He was a funny old guy, his face a sea of laugh lines. *Le Frontière* was his place, and most of its decorations came from his personal collection: holos he'd taken of the Frontier stars, rocks he'd picked up from dozens of worlds, pieces of burned-out machinery that had once been living components on his ship. They filled the display cases that ringed the big shop, hung on walls, even decorated the bathrooms. The seats were salvage, too, taken from various decommissioned ships. Somehow, all this stuff didn't make the place look cluttered. Erkki had an aesthetic eye.

"What's down, Kit?" His voice was a rasp, probably from years of barking out orders.

"Oh, I feel like things aren't gelling," I said. "Here I thought Fareedh would be the hard sell, but now Peter's dumping on everything. I thought he'd be excited about the Drive. *You* were."

Erkki grinned. "I'm not surprised," he said. "You and I have known Pete for ages. You're never going to get him fueled up by appealing to his sense of adventure. He doesn't have one."

The realization hit me. Peter wasn't worried about missing school. He was scared to leave home. He'd lived on Vatan all his life, and now I was asking him to explore the Frontier. I'd taken it for granted that anyone would jump at that chance, but not everyone is me.

I pursed my lips. "So what do I do?"

"He's a technician," Erkki said. "Engage that engineer brain of his."

I looked back at the table, at my three friends. Marta had shown interest. That was something. And I was sure I could count on Pinky, whenever he decided to show up. But if I couldn't convince Peter, I certainly wouldn't get Fareedh on board. Without those two, we were shipwrecked before we even started. I frowned. How could I turn this thing around?

"I see I got you thinking. That's good," Erkki said. He'd washed his hands and was wiping them on his apron. "In the meantime, what'll it be tonight? The usual?"

"Um...yeah," I said distractedly. "Oh, and a thing of sugar." I couldn't help grimacing. Who puts sugar in coffee?

"Pinky coming?" Erkki asked.

"Should be."

"I'll fix him something special."

"Thanks."

Erkki pinged my *sayar* for the bill. I felt it give a small buzz of acknowledgment in my pocket, one that would be mirrored on four other *sayar*s (with a 20% cut for Peter). I stepped aside for the next customer and waited, staring at the little mobile of colored plastic balls hanging over the counter. It was a big gold sphere surrounded by eight smaller ones in a bunch of different colors. I think they'd been salvaged from a LawnBall package and quick-painted. Not one of Erkki's more inspired decorations. Maybe a kid had given it to him or something.

Then a sudden hush came upon the place. The conversation flickered out, and even the musicians missed a beat. I knew what had happened without even turning my head.

Pinky had arrived.

The patrons stared, two dozen pairs of eyes locked on Pinky's odd form. I couldn't blame them.

Pinky was an alien.

He looked like something out of a nightmare, a half-melted sculpture of a man, mouthless and stocky, sauntering in on three thick legs. He padded through the cafe, ponderous and deliberate, an unsettling rhythm to his rolling gait. Raising a rubbery pseudopod, he hailed the gang at the table, not noticing me. His two eyespots were both currently on the front of the head-sized lump on top of his round body, and I wasn't in their field of view. As he moved toward the gang, chatter rose to compete with the musicians again, though it was a shadow of what it had been.

I waved to Erkki. He nodded acknowledgment, and went back to work. Aliens were nothing new for him. I followed Pinky on tiptoe, my breath held tight. Conversations remained subdued as patrons pulled in their legs and otherwise made sure to be out of his way as he purposefully lurched forward. This made it easier for me to dart ahead, trying to silently close the gap between us. Could I reach him before he got to the table? We were still a full three meters apart when the alien halted. I paused, still not breathing.

He must have smelled me.

He swiveled his eyespots 180 degrees before also turning his body, slowly, to face me, his smooth form flexing and stretching ominously. Pinky seemed to squint; the crooked spirals of his eyespots boring into me. Silence grew around us again, tense with anticipation.

And then he contracted like a bellows, making a deafening raspberry sound. Pinky waved a hand-like extension in an exaggerated motion and said in a perfectly human baritone, "Oh! Pardon me." He turned a bright crimson of embarrassment to match the gesture.

There was a moment of stunned quiet. Then, the snapped tension rebounded in laughter. Nervous at first, and then whole-hearted, contagious. The noise got so loud, the dampeners went into effect, stifling the echoing sound to a less deafening volume. A guitar string snapped, and I saw its owner double over his instrument. One customer actually fell out of her chair. Even Fareedh was smiling, one eyebrow raised, though Peter's expression was one of long-suffering.

I tried to keep my composure, biting my lip and attempting a frown. I lasted two seconds before the giggles won. I shook my head, smiling.

Pinky *always* had to make an entrance. At least he hadn't actually produced a bad smell to go with his act.

"When are you going to learn, Kitra," Pinky said, his voice coming from no one spot in particular, "that you'll never be able to sneak up on me?"

"There was that one time, when we were twelve..."

"A fluke."

"And last year, at the school dance..."

The alien blew a sound from his midsection in a perfect imitation of a snort. "I was just humoring you."

"Hah!"

"Well, just remember..." he said in mock menace, rotating his body while keeping his gaze on me, "Turnabout is fair play." Then he pulled out a chair and sat down, molding his bottom to the cushion, as the music and the conversations rose to their former level.

He spread his pseudopods expansively and asked, "So, when are we leaving?"

I sat down too, feeling a little better. Pinky was my oldest friend. I hoped he could salvage things.

Peter looked up at the alien. "Did she tell you about the Drive?"

"Last night," Pinky said. "You just found out?"

Peter nodded. "Yeah."

"It's pretty great, isn't it?"

"It's not what I signed up for." Peter's arms were still folded, his tone certain.

I looked at Marta, asking her with my eyes to do something, but she just shook her head. I couldn't expect her to force Peter to come along on my adventure. I felt the dream slipping away. I had to do something.

Erkki's words came back to me, and I nodded slightly to myself. I had to make Peter see the Drive as a science project, not as an untamed beast. Get him so interested in the physics that he'd set aside his fear of the unknown.

"Peter," I began, "Your said your biggest worry is missing school, right?"

He tilted his head. "Ye-es. That's what I said."

"And what's your major?"

"Multidimensional engineering. You know that..."

"Right," I nodded. "Well, look. I've seen the labs at the university. I know how it works. You only get two hours a week with a simulated Drive. Everything's theoretical."

"Yeah," he agreed. "It's a lousy system. So what?"

"Well, if you come with us, you get to work with a live Drive. One you have complete control over, one you can tailor to your exact specifications. No theory at all, it's the real thing."

Marta picked up on where I was going. "Peter, doesn't the school offer credit for experience? Like interning on a starship?"

"Well, sure, but--"

I pounced. "Don't you see? Why waste all those hours on a rented system when you could *have* the system? One that doesn't just simulate Jump space; it *gives* you Jump space. I'm not interfering with your plans. I'm speeding them up!"

He opened his mouth to respond, but it was clear that the last point had scored with him. His eyes unfocused for a moment as he thought it over.

Then he shook his head. "It won't work. Don't get me wrong. A guy in my boots would kill to have a hyperspace unit of their own.

Having the thing to myself would be...wow. I mean...I could..."
Peter's face betrayed his conflict, excitement wrestling with caution.
Caution won. "But look: understanding the theory and actually running the Drive in action are two different things. I'm liable to get us
all killed."

Right, which was his problem all along. Sure, I was willing to take
that risk, but obviously he wasn't. I tried to think of a response.

Fareedh beat me to it. "No. You won't." His calm voice cut through
the noise of the room.

Peter looked at him. "How do you know?"

"I've seen the crazy stuff you work on. I bet you could keep a
Drive calibrated in your sleep." He leaned forward and put his bony
elbows on the table, forearms over each other. "The tricky parts, going in and out of hyperspace, ending up where we're supposed to be,
that's not your job. It's mine and Pinky's." He fixed his dark eyes on
Peter's blue ones. "And we won't let you down."

Whoa. It wasn't *you* anymore. It was *we*. Finally!

"How can you be so sure?" There was no skepticism in Peter's
voice. It was a genuine question.

Fareedh gave him a lazy smile. "Because I'm the best."

Another pause. I looked at Peter. He looked down at the table.
Then he waved a hand at Pinky dismissively. "Well, what about him?
How's a blob supposed to be our navigator? They can't even see the
stars on their foggy world."

I flushed scarlet at the slur. It wasn't a nice thing to say, even kidding around.

If it bothered Pinky, he certainly didn't show it, not that anything ever seemed to faze him. He just crinkled the ends of his face in
his crude imitation of a smile. "Ah, but you forget. We 'blobs' know
where everything is in the universe."

"Is that so?" Peter asked. I knew what was coming. Oh, Peter.
Always the straight man.

"Yes," Pinky answered, swelling himself into even more of a ball-
shape and making a circle with his pseudopods, "we've all been a-
round."

Marta giggled. Peter wadded up a napkin and threw it at Pinky. It
bounced off his right "shoulder." "See, that's the real reason I wasn't

going to go. Three weeks cooped up with this guy?"

My heart jumped. I looked at him. "Wasn't? Past tense?"

He gave me a loud sigh followed by a smile. "Yeah. Past tense. You got me, like you always do. You and your crazy friends." Marta squealed, wrapped him in a hug, and kissed his cheek. I was sorely tempted to join her. Instead, I gave Fareedh a grateful smile. He winked at me. I had to admit, the boy was full of surprises. I'd had no idea he'd been sold on shipping out with us. If he hadn't come through when he did, the whole idea might have fallen apart.

"But I'm only committing to one trip," Peter went on after Marta let him go. "After that, it's my option whether I stay on or not."

I nodded. "Fair enough." I'd take what I could get.

Erkki's server, a thin young man I knew by sight but not by name, arrived with our orders on a shiny platter. He set it down in the center of the table. On it was a silver pitcher as well as five small cups, steam rising from them. My nose wrinkled. The fifth cup smelled like sandalwood and varnish remover. I pushed it in Pinky's direction. "I think this is yours," I said.

Pinky accepted the cup with a clumsy four-fingered hand. He made an exaggerated sniffing sound, the vapors disappearing momentarily into his fingers, then waved his other hand at the proprietor. He rolled his head back in mock ecstasy and called out, "Good choice, Erkki!" The old pilot nodded cheerfully in response.

I took a deep breath, appreciating the aroma and the rich head of foam on my coffee. Peter was mixing in a healthy pour from the sugar pitcher.

"This calls for a toast," I said, grabbing my cup and standing. The others joined me...except for Pinky, who just lifted his pseudopod and stretched it into the air until his cup was as high as ours.

"To being a crew!" Marta fluted.

"To a fun time," Fareedh drawled in reply.

Peter muttered, "To a twelve-month doctorate."

I looked down at Pinky. "Anything to add?"

"Oh no. I think I've said enough."

"Then...to a new beginning," I said. I took a sip, scalding my tongue a little.

It was perfect.

"Then…to a new beginning!"

Chapter 3

Eighteenth of Red, 306 P.S.V. (Launch -49 days (Standard))

By the time the sun had set, risen again, and was about to set once more, I realized I was in for a lot more than I'd bargained for. I paged through lines and lines of notes on my *sayar*, everything I could think of as being necessary for outfitting my new ship. I looked up from the screen, over the desk and out the open window of my bedroom. It faced north, so the long shadows from the trees and the fountain in the garden streamed rightward across the perfectly manicured lawn. Windchimes tinkled softly, hanging at strategic points around the green space. I had a pang of nostalgia, and for a moment, I half-saw Pinky, a fraction of his current size, running clumsily across the grass. He was never fast enough to catch me at tag, but he *always* found me when we played hide-and-go-seek.

I shook my head to clear it. So much to do! I went through the long list on my *sayar* again. It was a disorganized mess, and I worried I'd left something out, so I grouped what I'd written into a rough timeline. That helped.

I saw that some things could be started simultaneously: we could buy supplies while contractors patched up the holes in the hull and installed new engines and a power-plant. Making the inside livable and updating the bridge to modern standards couldn't be done until afterwards. A lot of this was work the five of us could do ourselves, but there was also much we'd have to leave to professionals. I sighed. More expenses.

I leaned back in my chair, rubbing the fingers of my right hand together as I thought. We couldn't expect to make any money on the shakedown cruise of an untested ship, so there were some tough decisions to make. My eyes unfocused, blurring the holos of planetscapes and explorers that lined my walls. What could we afford? Air was close to free, of course, and fuel almost as cheap as the water it came from. Food would cost a bit more. Other things like an air-car for scouting around on planets, advanced sensors, weapons, defenses — those were all luxuries that would probably have to wait for a while. This was going to be a bare-bones jaunt. Still, there was so much to plan. I hadn't even named the ship yet!

There was a knock at the jamb of my open door.

"Hello, Uncle," I said, looking up.

Aside from his ridiculous bushy mustache, Uncle Yusuf bore a strong physical resemblance to my mother. But Mom never wore his current expression, one of disapproval. At least, she had never showed it to me.

"You're really going through with it," he said, arms folded over his brocaded vest.

I braced for another fight. "I told you I would."

"Maryam wouldn't have wanted this."

"This is exactly what she'd want. It's what I want."

Uncle Yusuf opened his mouth to reply, closed it again, then simply said, "Very well." His eyes became opaque. "You're going to have to get your affairs in order. Establish beneficiaries and divest yourself of family obligations. Please do not neglect these duties." His tone was stiff. Final.

"But that'll take days," I said. "I need to work on the ship."

"You have made this decision," he said, folding his hands behind his back. "You knew what this would mean."

I looked down and nodded. Yes, I did. Going on this adventure meant abandoning Uncle Yusuf's plans for my future. He was not going to be responsible for me if I got myself killed out there, as his sister had. I wanted to be mad at him for being so unreasonable, but I found I had no anger in me. Uncle Yusuf wasn't a bad man. He was just scared.

I licked my lips. "Uncle?" When I looked up, he had already left. I found my vision blurred again, and I blinked to clear it.

Yes, I understood my uncle. But at the same time, I knew he was wrong. My ship and my friends *wouldn't* fail me. We would make it to the stars and back, safe and sound. And when we were done, the Yilmaz name would shine more brightly than ever before. I owed Mom that much. I gave the armrest of my chair a little thump, stared at the garden for a while.

Then I went back to looking over my list

Third of Queen, 306 P.S.V. (Launch -14 days, Standard)

The scout finally looked like a spacefaring vessel — from the outside, at least. A lot had gotten done in the last three-day week while I'd been away taking care of legal affairs. The foam and holes and ugly gray were gone. The ship's skin now gleamed an unbroken brilliant white. Its lines were beautiful, the aerodynamic curves of the hull seamlessly meeting the twin nozzles of the engine. Instead of the old, faded panels covering the big gap amidships, there was now a pregnant bulge: the new power plant. Her amber running lights, at the nose and on the wingtips, glowed cheerily, and a faint low hum filled the hangar. She was alive.

I pushed hair out of my face and tied it back. *We just might pull this off*, I thought.

I looked at the ship, *my* ship, and dreamed of horses. My mother had taught me about them and their history. They were native to old Earth and had been brought to many worlds, though none had ever set foot on Vatan. Long ago, owning a horse made one a noble. This ship was my steed, letting me gallop to the stars.

That made me something special. Most ships are owned by big companies, universities, or governments. A privately owned vessel that could travel between worlds, owned by someone as young as me, no less! I had the right to be proud.

I only wished I had a good name for it.

It's not that I hadn't thought it over. I'd actually given it a lot of consideration, but nothing seemed right. Looking at the now-sleek lines of the ship, I imagined it with a famous explorer's name emblazoned across its skin. Like *Magellan, Armstrong*, or *Ansari*. No, that could get awkward in communications: *This is Kitra Yilmaz of the Armstrong*. Or even *This is Armstrong*. It just sounded strange.

I thought about the suggestions the others had given me. Marta wanted to call the ship *Le Swan*, but horse metaphors aside, I didn't think an animal name was appropriate. The ship was bigger than that. I didn't want it trivialized. For the same reason, I didn't want a silly name, like Pinky's suggestion, *WingDing*. That was just stupid. The ship needed a grand name to match my plans for it. Like *Endeavour* or *Enterprise*. I needed to give it more thought.

Stairs led up into the ship. My footsteps echoed metallically as I went up the ramp to take stock of the interior. The ceiling panels of the lower corridor now radiated a warm glow, mimicking sunlight. Nothing had yet been done with the walls and floor, though. They were still dull and gray with preservation foam. I paused at the breach, nostrils flaring. The tang of the stuff was strong, competing with the smells of ozone and dust. It wasn't exactly unpleasant, but it always caught me off guard.

Going up a level, the main deck was almost starting to look homey. When we'd first gotten the ship, all the Navy had left us in the upper deck were two pairs of little state rooms, a bridge in front, and a big central area connecting them; all of them empty except for a centimeter of dust. It was up to us to not only make the space livable, but to turn it into a home away from home. Once we got going in earnest, we'd be here for weeks at a stretch.

Things weren't beautiful yet. They were barely even functional. The big central space was now partitioned into three rooms with raw new walls, circuit fabric forming frayed edges at their joins. I was already looking past the reality, though, imagining the walls whole and painted, with carefully chosen holos on them. I walked into the common area that filled the left side of the space, facing forward. We called it the "wardroom," a naval tradition. Long and narrow, it had a big table we'd all gather around when we were space-borne. No chairs yet, or decorations anywhere. The wall shelves I'd installed the week before were currently retracted and not visible, but Marta had finished setting up the little galley for making meals. It was actually kind of cute, with little reconstituters, a set of dishes, a small but functional bunch of utensils, and even heaters for cooking from scratch. All of us were bringing makings for our favorite dishes, and we planned to cook dinners for everyone in rotation. My mouth watered as I thought about Marta's sweet, cinnamon *korvapuustit* rolls. And Peter's *Gigot d'agneau* like his mother made, the lamb shanks dripping with garlicky goodness. And my…um…grilled cheese sandwiches. Well, I wasn't going to be captain for my cooking skills. In my defense, Pinky's were worse.

Doors opened on mine and Pinky's staterooms, and there was a double door that led to the bridge. There was also a door that Peter had installed opposite the staterooms. I went through and found myself in the workshop; it filled most of the other half of the central space. It was more or less complete, with a bench, a bed, a Maker, and several pieces of equipment. This was where we would fix or make new parts, mechanical or organic, if we ever needed to.

I opened up and peered inside the closet carved out of the back end of the workshop. The floor of the small room gleamed. This was probably the only time it would ever be empty. That was okay; you always need a place to throw your random junk.

Behind the wardroom were the two bays for big cargo. I took a quick look at the starboard one to my right. It was cleared out and ready to house an air-car, once I could afford one. They can be sealed up pretty good, and then they're practically little spaceships of their own, good for scouting or even as escape vessels. Without one, it was best to stick to settled systems and whatever public transit they had there.

I crossed the deck to the port bay and looked inside. It was full. Big boxes. Little boxes. Plastic and metal thingamajiggers, glittery control units. I didn't recognize most of it, but I knew who it had to belong to. I'd seen these kinds of piles before.

"Peter?" I called out. "Is this your junk?"

I heard an indecipherable mumbling from one of the tall stacks. I moved toward the sound, taking care not to trip over anything.

"What did you say?" I asked.

Peter's head appeared above a tower of boxes. "I said, 'No, it's yours.' "

"Come again?"

"This is mostly stuff that came out of the ship when they put in the new components."

I looked around, unable to recognize any of it. "I'm confused. We were told the Navy took out everything of value."

"You mean like the Drive?" Peter said with a quickly flashed smile. He walked around the tower to where I was. "In all seriousness, this is stuff that the Navy probably *meant* to leave, a lot of it in the walls themselves. I think it wasn't worth the effort to rip them out to salvage." He poked a coiled bit of wire gently with his foot. "Some of it's basic structural stuff we can't use like old socket junctures, obsolete panel conduit. But," his eyes glowed and he pointed to what looked like a big gray box inside a bronze birdcage, "I think this is a deep radar unit."

"I'll take your word for it," I said. "What are those big round things over there?" They stood out from the rest of the miscellaneous stuff.

"Oh, those are capacitors," he said. "Like big batteries. They probably charged the weapons bay."

My eyes widened. "Did they leave us beam cannon?!" The idea was not entirely pleasant. I don't like guns.

"I'm afraid not, hero." He folded his arms. "I might find a use for them, though. And we could get weapons someday." He didn't sound enthused at the prospect either.

I looked over the piles and realized there *was* some stuff that looked familiar. "What about these boxes? These things didn't come from the ship."

"No," Peter said, and smiled sheepishly. "You caught me. I also brought in my equipment. You never know what might be useful and," he looked a little more embarrassed, "it's cheaper to store it here than in a rental unit."

"Peter, we have limited space."

"I know, but if we're gallivanting around the system, we'll want all the spares we can carry. Especially while we're putting the ship through her paces. There's plenty of room if we're not shipping cargo. It's best to be prepared."

He was so into it now, way more like the Peter I knew than the skeptical guy I'd seen at the coffee house. Erkki'd been right. I just needed to give him a place to play with his toys. Impulsively, I patted his shoulder. "I'm really glad you decided to join us. I don't know what I would have done if you hadn't."

I saw his cheeks color. Then he tried to hide it by looking at the floor. "No problem. It's fun."

I waved at the clutter and said, "I assume you're cataloging all of this stuff?"

He looked up, following my gesture. "That's what I was doing when you called for me."

"Got it. All right." I smiled and said, crisply, "As you were."

Peter gave me an exaggerated mock salute. "Yes, sir, Captain Yilmaz, sir."

I shoved him gently and turned, heading for the bridge.

My breath caught as I entered the control room. There had been little here the last time. Now it looked…'eager' was the only word for it. Ready to go. Glowing panels lined the room in a rough horseshoe, and the Window filled the space above them, to the front and sides. I knew it was just a screen, and yet it seemed to be clear, unbroken glass, the walls of the hangar plainly visible through it. I sat down in the left chair, my chair. It shifted its contours to fit me comfortably. My panel blinked warmly at me, inviting my touch. I quickly found the controls for the Window's visual filters. One tap, and the hangar became a tracery of glowing lines and right angles. Another, and it disappeared, to be replaced by a fuzzy, monochrome image of the ground and sky. No buildings blocked the horizon. No clouds obscured the sun. That was pretty cool.

I looked back at the panel. The displays were active, streaming information on the ship's health. None of them were super important in and of themselves, but taken as a whole, we could read them like a doctor reads a patient's vitals.

My eyes were drawn to the middle of the panel. Right under the Window's center was a thin, branching constellation of red, yellow, and green lights labeled with the names of all the ship's subsystems: Environmental, Power Plant, Ship's *Sayar*, Engines, Drive, plenty more. I'd be able to tell the health of all the major ship's systems at a glance. I'm sure the array has a technical name, but I didn't know it. I decided to call it "The Tree."

To the right of The Tree was the internal layout display, a real-time blueprint of the ship. There was a glowing dot moving around in the port bay. Peter, if the map was showing people. I looked for me in the control room, and found my dot right way. Hmm. That was odd. It looked like there were two dots on the bridge, not one. I felt the muscles of my forehead knit.

"So nice of you to join me," I heard Fareedh say from no more than a meter away. I jumped with a small scream. I looked down, and sure enough, there he was, cross-legged on the floor next to the navigator's seat with a *sayar* in his hand.

I found my breath, heart racing. "You know, most of us use a chair."

He quirked an eyebrow and gave me that dreamy smile. "Overrated." He offered his hand, eyes fixed on mine. "Help me up?"

I rolled my eyes but helped him up anyway. He gave me a little bow, and then sat next to me in the right-hand chair. "Do you want to see what I've done?" He gestured to the set of physical and virtual controls jutting from the panel.

Curious, I groped for them. They seemed to meet me halfway, molding to conform exactly to my fingers. They were warm, alive. As my grip tightened, the room transformed. The lights dimmed and the displays now showed other information: altitude, speed, air pressure. A hundred other pieces of data that I, as pilot, would need to know.

"You did all this?"

He nodded, a satisfied smile playing on his lips. "Most of it."

He tapped his side of the panel a couple of times. The center of the Window returned to a view of the hangar wall, but on the left, partitioned by a pink line, I saw a shimmering marble of a planet. Vatan, mostly full, a thin crescent of night at one side. On the right of the Window, there was an overhead view of a city. I quickly recognized it as Denizli from the starport sprawling at its center.

"Is this live?" I asked, thrilled.

"Yes," Fareedh said. "While we're on the ground, we're hooked into the satellite web. In space, the ship's *sayar* goes off live observations or the latest data."

"Is it..." my pulse became strong in my temples again, "is the ship ready to fly?" I had a wild urge to punch the engine sequence and blow right through the hangar walls.

He chuckled. "Hardly. The new ship's *sayar* was installed last week, and it's online, obviously, but it's still not hooked into all functions." He ran his hand through his hair, but it stayed a mess. A cute mess, I decided.

"I've actually had to set everything up myself," he said. "It's an old ship. I had to set up a virtual sayar to run the original software just to get the ship to turn on. It's kind of a kluge, an old system running in the new ship's sayar."

"So we're running software from the old ship's *sayar*? That's almost a century old!" I turned to look at him.

"Underneath a modern operating system, yes," Fareedh admitted. "It's usable, though. Once I patch the connections. Plus, the old stuff came with a nice set of automatic navigation sequences."

I fiddled idly with the virtual buttons under my left hand, flipping through information screens in silence for a bit. Then, "You've done a great job."

He wiggled his eyebrows. "I aim to please..." he said smoothly.

I gave his hand a soft slap. He just leaned back in his chair and eyed me speculatively.

"What?" I asked.

"You were just so eager to go," he said. "I like that. And I promise I'll have ol' 'what's-its-name' ready in no time."

"It's just as well," I said. "I still haven't come up with anything better than 'what's-its-name'."

He gave me a wry smile. "We can't go off on an adventure without the ship having a name. It's bad luck."

"I know, I know," I said, waving my hand as if to swat away a fly. Then I paused in mid-wave. Of course. I should have thought of it sooner. 'Adventure'.

"That's it!" I cried.

Fareedh raised his eyebrows in query.

"*Majera*," I said brightly, using my parents' native tongue.

He blinked and was silent a moment. Then he quirked his lip and nodded. "Right. *Seikkailu, Aventur*," he said, translating *Majera* first into Finnish, then French, the language we normally spoke in.. "But why Turkish?" he asked.

"To honor my Mom."

He nodded, satisfied. "I like it."

"Me too!" I enthused, rubbing my palms together. "Just think how cool it'll be to say, 'This is *Adventure* calling...' In fact, I think I'm going to say that a lot."

Fareedh broke into a genuine smile, and he nodded encouragement.

I couldn't help smiling back. I felt a lot better. Picking a name finally put everything into place, made it real. And seeing Fareedh's grin, it was clear that under the flirting and the cool calculation, there was real enthusiasm. He was hooked. Between that and Peter happily working with his gear, well, now I knew we were all in it together. A real crew.

In one week, we'd be going on an adventure.

Going on *the Adventure*.

Chapter 4

Ninth of Wind, 308 P.S.V. (Launch Day)

"Three. Two. One. *Liftoff!*" My voice rang high with emotion as I punched the controls.

With a deafening roar, huge streams of fire erupted from *Majera*'s engines, their acceleration slamming me into my seat with twice my normal weight. Flames streaked past the Window, the gees increasing until I felt the full force of seven gravities crushing the air out of me. My vision blurred until I could hardly see the Window, or Pinky seated next to me. Faster and faster we went, the rickety hull threatening to shake itself to pieces. There was the violent *snap* as external booster rockets fell away, then a jerk as our main engines turned off, and we floated weightless in orbit.

At least, that's how it had always been in the historical romances I read.

The launch was nothing like that. These days, ships don't launch — they levitate. I think we've lost something.

Watching the ground drift away through the *Majera*'s Window, I recalled all the times I'd flown in my glider, that feeling my stomach got when I climbed or dove or turned. That little clench in my diaphragm and the spinning in my inner ear that connected me to my machine and what it was doing. The gentle pressure on my back when I sped up, the thrill as I careened around in a tight bank. Acceleration.

Now, there was none of that. There was no sensation of movement at all, in fact. And yet, the view through the Window made it clear that we *were* moving, the ship's anti-gravity thrusters shooting us upward at a steady rate. I angled the view downward and watched the spaceport dwindle to a gray asterisk, to a dot, to an indistinguishable point inside the sprawling capital. Soon after, the city was gone, too. The bright sun turned the nearby sea into a lake of fire. The river was a shimmering silver ribbon.

The sky gently changed colors, from pale blue to navy to indigo to black. In just ten minutes, we were clear out of the atmosphere, two hundred kilometers up. I could see the curve of the horizon and the stretches of silver, brown, and green that made up Vatan's surface. It was a pretty view and yet, I felt detached. There was no sense of vertigo or that tingling in my fingers I still sometimes got when looking down from a height. There was hardly any sound. Just the quiet hiss of the air blowers and the breathing of five beings. Despite everything, I found myself a little disappointed. We might as well have been watching a recorded holo of a liftoff rather than making one.

Wait a minute. I reached out to turn off the cabin lights and dim the displays, plunging us into almost complete darkness. I expanded the Window to cover most of our field of view. My heart skipped a beat.

In the dark, the view was brilliantly beautiful.

Thousands of stars, constant and as bright as anything. They crowded together tightly, far too many to count. I felt like I could read by their light, that's how brilliantly they shone. Vatan's nearer moon was a dazzling, featureless ball, just above the curve of the planet. Behind it, a glowing arch soared from the planet's surface into the heavens: Vatan's rings.

My tongue was dry, and I realized my mouth was open. I closed it and swallowed.

I swiveled my chair completely around. Peter, Marta, and Fareedh were ghosts in the low light. Sitting in low-slung temporary couches, Peter's and Marta's behind mine, and Fareedh's behind Pinky's, they had access to their own panels along the side of the Bridge. The small room was crowded, but at least it fit all of us.

I cleared my throat and pointed a thumb over my shoulder. "Some view, huh?"

Peter nodded, his eyes wide. "Uh huh."

I kicked his shoe lightly. "Too late to turn back now, hmm?" I teased. Then I added, "Thanks again for making the party."

"Well, all of my stuff is here," he answered. But his grin glinted in the starlight.

I turned back to the Window, and tried to find the destination I wanted, but it was lost among the bright stars. "Pinky," I said. "Where's Four?"

A moment later, one of the brightest of the "stars" got a green circle around it and a curved blue line arced out from the bottom of the Window to meet the circle. It was obviously a planet, now that it was pointed out. It had a yellowish tinge and was big enough to just barely show as a disk instead of a point. A small gas giant, 40 million kilometers away, officially named Bilye. Everyone just called it Four.

I brought the lights up and shrank the Window a bit. Now I could only see the brightest stars. I took a deep breath, finally feeling the excitement the moment deserved.

"All right," I said. "Let's have the first status report of the trip. How are we looking?"

"The power plant is running at expected levels," I heard Peter say. "The engines are warm and ready for action. Hydrogen fuel tanks are full up."

Marta's voice chimed in. "No leaks in the hull, and the environmental systems are online. Air reserves are at maximum. Water reserves are at maximum."

"Pinky's at maximum," my friend wheezed. I looked at him, and sure enough, he had made himself too big and round for his chair, which was literally struggling to accommodate him. Pinky: King of visual puns.

"You know," I chided. "It'd help if you stuck to one shape."

Pinky shrugged three arms. "Where's the fun in that?"

I glanced over at The Tree. All of the active systems were tinted a healthy green. The symbols for things we didn't have, the weapons bay and the multi-use pod, were a dull brown.

"Ship's *sayar* is online and all functions are, um, functioning," Fareedh said. "The link to the old system is working fine, as is the modern interface on top of it."

He'd done a great job. All of the displays used familiar fonts and setups. It was hard to believe that underneath the patches, the *Majera*'s software was decades old.

"What do you think, Pinky? Can you get us to Four with Fareedh's kluge?" I gave Fareedh a smile over my shoulder so he knew I was only teasing him. Unfazed, he blew me a kiss. I rolled my eyes, but I had to turn to hide a blush.

Pinky ran three thick fingers across his control panel. A moment later, he said breezily, "Course laid in." He looked at me and added, "At one standard gee of acceleration, I can have us there in 1.48 standard days. That'd be…0.69 Vatan days. At two gees, we can be there in…1.05 standard days." Pinky was showing off, not using a *sayar* to do his math.

"With full tanks, I don't see why we wouldn't do two gees," I said. "Peter?"

"Yeah. That's a safe thrust for a long stretch," he said.

"You got it, boss." Pinky manipulated his panel, and *Majera*'s engines came to life. I felt, more than heard, the faint thrum from the engines. I turned the Window's focus back to Vatan so we could watch it go. The reflections off the ice covering a third of the planet made it glitter. After a few minutes, Vatan was just a soccerball sized sphere painted in turquoise and white.

"It's kind of…I don't know." Marta said, breaking the silence. "Somehow, I'd thought taking off for our first journey would be more dramatic." I had to smile. Now *she* was feeling the same way I had.

"If you like," Pinky said, "I could make the trip more exciting." He played with the anti-gravity controls before I could stop him, and I felt the floor lurch like we were being pitched on a rolling sea. Marta whooped with surprise. I gripped my chair as we careened right and left. It was a good thing we had seat harnesses.

"What are you doing?" Peter yelped.

"He's making the experience more cinematic," Fareedh said calmly. "Let me help." He started making loud whooshing sounds in time with the ship's rocking.

"You're not helping, guys," I said through gritted teeth. "Stop messing with my baby."

Pinky stopped clowning around, which was good because I was about to wallop him on his…well, I was about to wallop him. The floor ceased its rolling.

Marta pulled herself gently from her couch and smoothed her yellow dress; not the most practical thing for shipboard life, I noted, but it did look pretty on her. It was a lot classier than the casuals the rest of us were in, though I liked Fareedh's rainbow T-shirt.

"Tell you what," she said. "Why don't we celebrate our liftoff away from the controls." She glared at Pinky, who averted his eyespots, pretending shame.

I turned to watch as Vatan slowly shrank in the view. Part of me was reluctant to leave the bridge just half an hour into the flight. On the other hand, there wasn't all that much to *do* until turnover, the halfway point at which we'd flip the ship around and run our engine in the opposite direction, slowing down until we reached our target. Even that could be done automatically. Once the course was laid in, flying through space was easy. The excitement would happen at the destinations. Any fun we had in-flight, we'd have to provide for ourselves. We might as well start now.

"That *is* a good idea," I said at last. "Let's try out the new wardroom." I turned to urge everyone out of the control room only to find that everyone had already left, even Pinky.

I unclipped my belt, feeling a little down. Maybe space travel was going to be more dull than I thought. I couldn't even keep my crew on the bridge for half an hour. I got up and went through the double doors.

The loud "SURPRISE!" as I walked into the wardroom almost startled me out of my skin.

Somehow, in the time I'd spent alone on the bridge, the others had not only managed to get into the room, but to decorate it with banners, balloons, and streamers. No, they must have set this up earlier, before they'd taken their stations. There was even a blue cake on top of the big table's center, flames dancing at the end of a bunch of candles. The cake was shaped like...I don't remember what they're called. Some kind of sea mammal with flippers and smooth skin. It had giant, lopsided eyes and a goofy smile drawn in dark icing.

"You guys," I said, shaking my head. "I can't turn my back on you for a second."

"This is a big deal," Marta said with a cheerful smile. "It calls for a real celebration. So I baked a real cake."

"Yes," Pinky said, stiffening and narrowing so that he was as tall as he could get, his head almost level with mine. He made a fair imitation of a throat-clearing cough and gestured dramatically at the pastry with all three hands. "This is our Seal of Approval," he said solemnly.

I clamped my lips, refusing to dignify the pun with a response. Not a laugh. Not a groan. Nothing. I caught a glimpse of the crooked grin on that stupid cake's face, the candle on its head slowly leaning from the flame's heat. It fell over. Smoke rose from the seal's nose. A snort flew past my lips, and then I was shaking in a laugh I couldn't stop.

Marta pointed an accusing finger at Pinky. "It was *his* idea."

"No it wasn't," Fareedh said proudly. "It was mine. Pinky just insisted on saying it." I shook my head slowly in disbelief, still laughing. Lord. *Two* Pinkys would drive Peter crazy.

I recovered, and Pinky offered me a translucent knife. "Care to do the honors?"

"Yes," I said. "But hold on one second. There's something missing." I squeezed past him to get to my door. The light went on as I walked into my room. It was still a mess. I hadn't set up anything but the bed, and all of my stuff was in boxes. I rummaged through them. Clothes. Hangers. Toiletries.

Pinky called out, "Hurry up! The candles are all melting."

"Coming!" I yelled. I carefully moved piles of stuff until I found the box I had been searching for, and then took the whole container without bothering to unpack its contents.

Fareedh and the others were already seated by the time I returned. I put the box on the table and tapped the release. The sides folded away revealing a set of six coffee cups, delicately painted and lacquered.

"Oh, they're beautiful!" Marta said.

"Yeah. My mom's," I explained. "I thought they'd be good luck. And you can't have sweets without coffee."

The cake was in danger of third-degree burns at this point. I bent over the table and blew out the candles. Then I took the knife Pinky had offered me and began careful surgery on the poor animal, although it's hard to cut equal slices when your cake isn't properly square. Marta and Fareedh chose pieces of the mid-section for their plates. Peter took *both* hindfins. I pushed the poor dissected creature's head onto my own plate, laughing evilly as I did. Pinky just expanded his hand, enfolding one of the seal's shoulders. It slowly disappeared into Pinky's porous skin.

The carafe heated as I grabbed it from the galley counter. By the time I poured the coffee, it was steaming. Taking a seat, I tucked into my piece of cake. It was amazing, carrot spice cake with dried purples. I chewed contentedly, admiring our little meeting room with its sky blue ceiling and grass-colored floor. There was real green, too, since Marta had set up containers at the room's corners, and they all had big broadleaf plants spilling out of them. Seeing them, I breathed deeply. The air seemed fresher than in the Bridge, though it might have just been my imagination.

"So, what's the plan, Kitra?" Peter set down his plate. He'd already finished. "Why'd you pick Four for the first stop?"

I swallowed my current bite and shrugged. "It seemed as good a spot as any. I'm open to other ideas." I dug in my pocket for my *sayar*. Tapping the device, I projected a map of the two stars in our system: Vatan's golden sun, Yeni Izmir, and its distant little red companion, Tuncay. There were six circles around the first, two around the second — planetary orbits.

"What have we got for options, Pinky?" Peter asked.

"Well…" The alien spread out a hand and started counting on his fingers. "Four's got a couple of moons we could visit. I think there's a big botanical garden on one of them." He looked over at Marta, but she didn't seem interested. "There's Lananina," he said, gesturing toward the fifth planet. "That's fun if you like ice sculptures. Some rocks in the asteroid belt might be worth visiting, especially if the Games are on. Three's got those luxury Ring Hotels."

"Which we can't afford," Fareedh noted.

"Right. Let's see…" He was out of fingers, so he grew a new one. "We could do a trip out to Garrison Station around Six, just to say we did. If the Navy'd let us land."

Marta looked doubtful. "None of those sound like exotic, exciting places. Isn't it kind of a waste of a starship not to, you know, go to another star?" She took a small bite of cake, swallowed, and added, "I wanted to get a Sennetian."

I looked at Marta blankly.

"It's a handbag," she explained. I shrugged.

Peter spoke up. "I don't think we should try the Drive just yet. The ship is untested, and besides, the in-system places don't sound so bad." He looked at Marta and said, "If we want to see another star, could we make it all the way to Tuncay? Just on engines, I mean."

I could tell Peter was having second thoughts, being his usual cautious self. "That's a long way," I said. "How long would that take, Pinky? Assuming Peter can keep us at two gees the whole way?"

"64 standard days," Pinky answered swiftly.

"Yeah," I said. "Nine standard weeks. That's too long. We'd probably run out of fuel."

"We'd certainly be out of food," Marta said. "Eight weeks is about our limit when we're fully stocked, and we're not."

We were all quiet for a bit. Fareedh's soft voice cut in. "So, the stars are out. Unless we use the Drive." He looked at me, eyes glowing. "The question is, will we on *this* trip?"

I thought about that for a second. As happy as I was to have gotten a ship with a Drive already installed, I hadn't really considered going on an interstellar trip the first time out. But now that we were talking about it...

I looked at the ceiling again and zoomed out the star map's scale to three parsecs, the safe range of our drive. There were twenty yellow, orange and red dots, stars, in fifteen systems including the big one representing Sennet, the province's capital. They winked at me temptingly. All of them were within reach of a single Jump once we got far enough from Vatan to switch on the Drive. Why not?

I bit my lip. No. We weren't ready. A million things can go wrong on a spaceship, and it didn't make sense to try to do everything at once. Besides, Peter was right. There *were* plenty of fine places to visit right here in our home system. What could it hurt to see the local sights before galloping off into the unknown? Or at least the less known. Adventure could wait a week.

I cleared my throat. "I think we should stay close to home for now. Let's learn to walk before we r – "

Red lights came on and klaxons sounded deafeningly in my ears, cutting off my answer. There was a lurch followed by the sound of creaking metal, as if the ship were groaning in pain. Out of nowhere, I felt a sharp punch to the gut. Marta and Fareedh doubled over, their faces contorted. Pinky belched a cloud of white gas. Peter had the worst of it. He threw up all over the table.

Moments later, the cramps left as suddenly as they'd come. I sat there for a moment, puzzled. Then my throat went dry as I realized what had just happened.

Oh, crap.

Chapter 5

Fareedh lurched clumsily toward the bridge. I looked over at Marta, who was grabbing a wipe for Peter. She gave me a nod, letting me know she had things under control, and I got up to follow Fareedh. In the control room, I found him sitting in his temporary chair, staring, his face paler than I'd ever seen it before. I followed his eyes...and froze.

The Window was empty.

Vatan was gone. The stars were gone. There wasn't even the honest blackness of space. It was a solid sheet of gray. No, gray is the wrong word for it. Gray is a color. What I saw was a kind of nothing, and *Majera* was surrounded by it. Even blurred and translated through the ship's systems, the nothingness clawed at the edges of the Window and threatened to eat everything around it: panels, chairs, hull. It dug into my brain, terrifying, but I also couldn't look away.

I had to turn the Window off, I knew that. But I couldn't move. My lips were set tightly. I couldn't even blink. I felt my hands balled into fists, trembling. It felt like, if I didn't act now, I would be lost in the grayness. I poured every gram of will I could into my right arm and lashed out, pounding at the panel. Thank goodness my aim was true. The Window flickered off, and the room suddenly felt very small.

I rubbed my throbbing hand. I'd have a hell of a bruise, but at least it was real pain, not that gut-wrenching nothingness that had paralyzed me and Fareedh. Pinky slid past me, having been there for who knows how long. He took his seat and began tapping at the panel, calling up a navigation map. Blank. He turned a deep maroon with puzzlement while expanding the range. Still nothing. "Kitra," he said, "there's no *there* there. Vatan, Four, even Yeni Izmir. They've vanished." He looked at me. "We're…"

"Yeah. In Jump," I finished. "I guessed it when the cramps hit."

Fareedh wheezed out a breath, his face now only a shade lighter than its normal deep tan. "I've never Jumped before. Is it always that bad?"

I nodded my head. "Yes. When we were kids, they always strapped us in and gave us meds." Exactly what I'd planned to do if and when we ever Jumped. "Fareedh, you were the first one here. Did you know what had happened?"

He looked back at his panel. "It's got to have something to do with the ship's *sayar*," he said. "But I don't know what triggered the Jump. I'll need a minute."

I closed my eyes, my mind wobbly. I felt out of control, like I'd woken up on a gravcoaster with no memory of even having gone to the fun park.

First things first. "Pinky, can you tell where we were when we went into Jump?" I asked. "Were we far enough away from Vatan?"

He nodded his stumpy head. "Way ahead of you," Pinky said, pointing to his panel. It was still showing the navigation map, but this time, all of the familiar spacemarks were on it. Vatan, the moons and rings, and our path from the planet, which ended in a big yellow dot marking where the Jump happened. "About 50,000 kilometers out from Vatan. Right at the edge of the safe zone."

"That's something, at least." If we'd been inside that limit… well, I didn't know what happened to ships that try to Jump too close to a planet. No one did.

"What is our destination?" I asked.

Pinky tapped at his panel with oversized fingers. Then, "I haven't a clue. The navigation *sayar* doesn't have a course laid in. *I* didn't do this." He sounded indignant. "Nav controls are locked, and I'm not picking anything up on our sensors." Pinky looked at me. "We're definitely in hyperspace."

Marta came in then, a green-faced Peter in tow. His eyes widened when he saw the panel, and I followed his gaze. He was looking at The Tree: the little icon representing the Drive wasn't just green, it was glowing brightly. "What did you do, Kitra?" He didn't wait for an answer. Instead, he pulled out his personal *sayar*, hooked up to

Majera's, and began to page through screens. He looked up at me, ashen. "The Drive is on."

"We know," Pinky and Fareedh said at the same time.

I almost laughed, the situation was so ridiculous. I felt light-headed. "Peter, can you tell if the Drive is working right?"

He fiddled with his *sayar*, then put it back in his pocket and worked directly at his bridge panel for a while. Finally, the furrow in his forehead relaxed slightly. "Yeah, actually," He sounded surprised. "No errors. All readings within normal range."

There wasn't any imminent danger, then. Alright. My heart was still galloping. That needed to stop so I could think more than a few seconds ahead. I focused on my breathing, like I did when things got particularly hairy on a glider flight. Two good breaths. In, out. In, out. Peter looked at me expectantly.

"Something tripped the Drive switch somehow," I said slowly. "The important thing to do now is find out where we're going."

"Yeah," Fareedh said, still agitated. "I'm checking the program. There must have been something preloaded." His thin fingers flew across his panel. I tried looking over his shoulder, but I couldn't make heads or tails of the torrent of words and shapes that flowed on the device's projected screen. I dropped into my seat and waited.

Peter looked up from his panel and said, his voice quavering slightly. "Kitra, our fuel is nearly half gone." He swallowed. "This could be a max-range Jump."

More bad news. It meant that we'd be running on empty when we left Jump. Still... "That's okay so long as there's a place to fuel up on the other side," I said. I tapped my armrest impatiently. "Fareedh?"

"Yeah, just a second." That was the first time I'd ever heard annoyance creep into his voice. I sat tight. Marta gave Peter a reassuring squeeze and ran her fingers through his hair.

Finally, Fareedh looked up, his expression flat. "There's nothing in the system that I can find. We didn't set the program, the logs don't show that we gave a command. It must have been caused by something deep in the original software." He was keeping his voice deliberately calm, but I could tell it was an effort. "It'll take me a while to find it...and I'll have to find it or this could happen again."

"Never mind that," Peter said, a vein throbbing in his temple.

"What happens if we Jump into empty space, 10 light years from home?"

Pinky's shrug was three-shouldered. "We might go nowhere at all," he said soothingly. "We didn't set any coordinates. We may just spend a week in hyperspace and pop out right next to Vatan."

"Why don't we find out where we are now?" Marta wanted to know. "Why can't we just turn off the Drive?"

"No!" Peter exclaimed. Then, slightly calmer, "That's just how it is. Once you're in Jump, you can't leave. You're in it for a week."

"6.89 standard days," Pinky said softly. I raised a finger to quiet him.

"Yeah, whatever," Peter said, waving his hand dismissively. "Point is, you can't stop in the middle. You'd just stay in hyperspace forever."

"Well...that's not so good," Marta said. "The ship's only got a week or two of food." At my look, she got defensive. "Hey, I didn't know this was going to happen. This wasn't supposed to be a long trip. Besides, I assumed we were going to fly where there were places to restock. Hell, I *thought* we were going somewhere I could *shop*."

I took a deep breath and exhaled in a rush. "Okay," I said. Then I stood up and faced them, trying to put on a convincing smile. "Look, there's no reason to assume the worst. The Drive works just fine, and hyperspace is about the safest place you can be. After all, there's literally nothing here. Fareedh will figure out where we're going." I looked at him for support. He nodded, but it was half-hearted. I forged ahead anyway. "We've got plenty of air, right, Marta?"

"I'll want to make sure all the recyclers are working right. Again, I didn't plan for a long trip."

"We can last a week, at least?"

Her round face brightened. "Oh yes. No problem. Probably two."

"Great!" I said a little too loudly.

"We should take stock of our stores," Marta went on. "I bet if we're creative, we can make things last."

I nodded in what I hoped was an encouraging manner. "Exactly. A week out, we'll fuel up, a week back, and done. Things are going to be just fine."

I sounded a lot more confident than I felt.

Launch Plus One (Standard)

I was at the end of a long, metal-plated hallway that stretched out endlessly in front of me. Everything was big and wide, filled with dark shadows. A starship as seen through the eyes of a kid, which I'd been the last time I'd seen space. The setting was familiar: the emissary cruiser I'd spent half of my childhood in. Mom's ship. I was half aware that I was dreaming, but not enough to wake up.

The school bell was ringing. I was late for class—again. I ran down the hallway looking for the classrooms we used when we were away from Vatan for months on end, but all the doors were dark and I couldn't remember where it was. None of the other kids were around. The bell got louder. I realized I hadn't done my homework for this session. In fact, now that I thought about it, I hadn't done my homework all *year*. I couldn't even remember what class I was supposed to be going to!

At some point the school bell became an alarm. Men and women were running past me, all carrying purple duffel bags. I stopped and looked at them in confusion. No, they were babies. Babies in purple space bags, disposable suits that don't have arms or legs. There was a loud crash, the sound of an explosion, and the deck lurched against my feet. I threw out my hands against an impact, but instead of falling down, I floated. So did everyone else. Purple bundles bounced off the walls and ceilings, and they began to wail at the same pitch and rhythm as the alarm. Cry Cry Cry, pause. Cry Cry Cry, pause. The noise grew louder, deafening, and I covered my ears. There was another explosion, and the sound of metal being tortured slowly out of shape. I watched in horror as the ceiling opened up, revealing the blackness of space. I felt myself drawn upward and outward into vacuum...

...I woke to the sound of birds chirping, my dream receding in foggy shards. Cheep cheep cheep. I blinked, confused. Cheep cheep cheep. I was in bed. When had I gone to bed? Cheep cheep cheep. My *sayar*! I got it out from under the pillow and focused bleary eyes onto its screen. Why was Fareedh calling in the middle of the night?

I thumbed the call active. "Hello?" I croaked.

"Kitra?" I could barely hear Fareedh's soft voice.

"Yeah." I cleared my throat. "Yeah, I'm awake. What's going on?"

"Sorry to wake you," he said. "I thought you were on the bridge."

"I was…no, I went to bed eventually." I remembered now.

"I think I figured out what happened," he said.

That woke me up faster than coffee. "Oh?"

"It's easier if I show you."

"Sure. Just a second," I said. There was the low tone that meant he'd cut the call. I rubbed the sleep out of my eyes and shivered. My dreams hadn't mirrored my memories so closely in a long time. I walked over to the wall to pull out the sink and splash some water on my face. I caught a glimpse of myself in the mirror and flinched. My hair looked like some kind of wild tentacled sea creature. There were bags under my eyes, too. I couldn't go out looking like this.

Then I shook my head and laughed. I was on a ship in the middle of nowhere in the middle of the night! Who cared what I looked like? Still, I attacked my hair with a brush, taming it into submission. The result was even kind of attractive, I decided. Sleep had set it in subtle waves. Good enough for 2 AM, at least.

My stomach rumbled as I left my cabin and entered the wardroom. The rice dish Fareedh had cooked everyone had been delicious but not very filling. I thought about raiding the Preserve for a snack, then considered where we were and what was going on and decided I could stand going a little hungry.

I snuck a glance at the bridge. The lights were on and most of the displays were going. The Window was still off, of course. Pinky was in his seat, sort of. He had absorbed all of his limbs and was almost a perfect ball. That generally meant that he was asleep. The lucky guy could sleep anywhere. I decided not to wake him and passed through the shop to knock quietly at the metal portal of the stateroom closer to the front of the ship. I didn't want to wake up Peter and Marta, who shared the cabin next door. A moment later, Fareedh, wearing the most garish tie-dye patterned pajamas, opened the door. His hair was a crazy mop.

It was kind of adorable.

"Hey, Captain," he said. He wore a shy smile, different from the knowing smirks he usually favored. I liked it better. "Sorry to wake you, but I thought you'd want to know sooner rather than later."

"That's okay," I said. "What's up?"

He stepped inside the jamb of the door and waved me in. I accepted the invitation.

Fareedh's cabin was just as small as mine: if he lay in the middle with his legs and arms outstretched, his fingers and toes would brush the walls. Still, he'd managed to turn the cramped space into a surprisingly homey place. There were soft wall-hangings with weird geometric patterns and soft-edged shapes that seemed to flow when you looked at them. Maybe they did; it was hard to tell in the muted light. They gave the room an illusion of greater space. Fareedh's bed was a low futon set with green, blue, and purple pillows. Next to them lay his *sayar,* three glowing displays hovering in an open trapezoid above it. There was the rich aroma of good tea brewing. An acoustic guitar lay propped up, caseless, in a corner.

I liked it here.

Fareedh set himself down on his bed, crossing his lanky legs. "Sit down and help yourself," he said, pointing. There was a little self-powered samovar beaded with moisture along with a few cups at the foot of the bed. I sat in the cabin's one chair and poured a cup. My feet dangled an inch off the deck—the seat was adjusted for Fareedh's height.

I looked at Fareedh over the steam curling upward from my cup. "So, what happened?" I asked.

He looked down. "This is my fault," he said simply. Gone was his confidence, his carefree swagger. He seemed a different person.

"What? How?"

"You remember that *Majera* runs on the old ship's *sayar* with the original software, but I had to run it through an emulator since the operating system is new, right?"

"Sure, of course. You said you had to patch in all the ship's functions manually."

"Right. Well." He lifted his head, his eyes very dark. "I missed one."

That sounded bad. I said so.

Fareedh stretched, joints popping. He pointed to the central screen above his *sayar* glowing with a bright green pattern. "That's the ship's nervous system," he said.

"It looks like a spider," I noted.

"Yeah. The body's the operating system. And the legs are all the connections."

I studied the diagram. The glowing spider was trapped in a *Majera*-shaped cage, the ship's components marked off as glowing purple boxes. Each of the legs went to the various ship's systems: Engines, Drive, Life Support, Navigation, some others. Between the boxes and the end of all of the legs was a black dotted line labeled "emulator wall." No, not all of the legs, I saw. One of them, drawn in yellow, went to a box that was split in half, with one side on the other unblocked side of the wall. It was cryptically labeled "Legacy Routines."

"I don't understand," I said through a yawn. "Excuse me." I took a tentative sip of tea. It was scalding, and perfect.

"It was a really foolish mistake. I'd been seduced by the Navy's otherwise straightforward and logical code," he said. "The emulator I set up worked the way it was supposed to, acting like a translator between the old software and the new operating system," he said. "I even integrated the navigation routes stored in the old system with the emulator so we'd have them if we wanted them. And that was the problem. When I went through the legacy stuff, it seemed to be all data with no active sequences. Just a kind of library." Fareedh leaned forward, his voice rising. "There was a set of subroutines buried in there, probably added as a patch by someone other than the original programmer."

I frowned. "What did those subroutines do?"

"I haven't cataloged all of them, but the one we triggered was set to run a Nav routine under certain circumstances. Point of origin and velocity, mostly. Whoever had this ship last probably put in the patch to save time; there'd be no need to even set a course. The ship would know where to go."

I was starting to understand. "So we matched the parameters to trigger this subroutine."

He nodded. "Right. We lifted off from Denizli, set the course for Four, and then activated the autopilot. As soon as we were the minimum safe distance from Vatan, this old subroutine used a back-end channel I didn't even know existed to tell Navigation to throw us into Jump using the coordinates it had stored."

"Lord," I whispered. Then the scope of the problem dawned on me. "Could there be little boobytraps throughout the system, not just Nav?"

"I've been doing a full audit, and I don't think so. The other systems check out as unaltered stock, as they did when I validated them while setting up the emulator. The only real customization was with the Nav routines." He sighed. "I just missed it. I thought it was just data," he repeated.

A thought occurred to me. "If the ship's *sayar* sent us somewhere, the coordinates for our destination should be in memory. We should know where we're going, right?"

Fareedh made a clicking sound with his tongue accompanied by a shake of his head. "I don't have a clue, actually."

My stomach sank further.

He went on. "We didn't set any coordinates, so the new system just says we're going nowhere. And here, this is what I see when I try to read coordinates from the old subsystem." He tapped his *sayar*, and one of the floating screens became a jumble of random numbers and letters. "That might have meant something to the original coder, but it's meaningless to me."

"Maybe Pinky could figure it out."

"That was my first thought. His math is obviously better than mine."

I wrinkled my nose. "No luck?"

"No."

"Um," I looked at him. "Is there any good news?"

"Yeah." Fareedh tapped at his *sayar* and a new dotted line crossed the yellow spider leg prior to the split box. "That should cut off any of the legacy routines. It means no autopilot, and of course we'll have to program all the Jumps by hand." He looked down from the floating diagram, meeting my eyes. "Again, I'm sorry, Kitra." He sounded exhausted. For the first time, I noticed the dark bags under his eyes that the dim light had hidden.

I set down my cup and instinctively put a hand on his shoulder. "Hey. It's okay. You did just fine. At least we know what went wrong.

Besides, Pinky wasn't going to trust our Jump to the ship's *sayar* anyway."

Fareedh looked a little more like himself again, straightening his back and giving me a grateful smile. We sat like that for a bit. It was quiet except for the gentle gurgle of the samovar. Fareedh glanced at my hand, still gripping his shoulder. I withdrew it, blushing.

"Thanks," he said. He looked at me seriously. "I won't let you down again."

I looked at Fareedh with new appreciation. I'd known him for a year, and yet I'd never felt like I understood him. If he wasn't flirty, he was aloof. Charming, sure. Handsome, absolutely. But always... removed.

He was different now. The mask, the arrogance was gone, and underneath, well, I liked what I saw. On impulse, I leaned forward and kissed his cheek. His eyes widened with surprise. I patted his hand and stood up. Even though he remained seated, we were still almost eye-to-eye, that's how mismatched our heights were. "Get some sleep, Fareedh. You've done what you can." I walked to the door and looked at him over my shoulder. "Thank you," I said, and meant it. I knew I could count on him.

"Things are different now…"

Chapter 6

Launch Plus Two (Standard)

The game had been my idea, to occupy our minds through the long week in Jump. There just wasn't much else to do: Fareedh had finished his audit and given up trying to unscramble the Nav coordinates we were headed to. Peter's data logging for the Drive was an automatic thing. Marta monitored the air system and made sure her plants were fed and watered. Pinky and I had literally nothing to do: in Jump, there are no stars to navigate by, and no way to change course, besides.

So I suggested a game.

I looked warily across the wardroom table at Marta. She was half-obscured by the brilliant map of the galaxy between us, but I could still make out that canny expression that always suggests impending mischief. I saw Fareedh catch her eye from the other end of the table, clearly trying to communicate something without words. I looked a question at him, and he began to gesture.

"No diplomacy during the execution phase," Pinky said matter-of-factly.

I blushed and looked down at my *sayar*. I'd been dithering over my turn for a while now. I repositioned myself in the chair to get blood moving again and was rewarded with pins and needles along the length of my calves. How long had we been at this game? I tapped the *sayar*, checking the time. Wow. We'd been playing *Empires* for the better part of eight hours already. And four hours the day before.

Empires was a simulated war for control of the galaxy, with each player controlling a different star league. We'd blown endless off-days (and not a few school nights) on it back before graduation. It had been fun in its original form, but over the years, we'd made our own rules and customizations for it, expanding the races and tech options to suit our styles and keep up with the times. Like when the Empire discovered the Bugs our Second Year, only the third race of aliens humans had ever encountered. They saw in five dimensions, and they'd probably have been rulers of the galaxy if they'd ever left their planet. Fareedh had added them, and they were his favorite species to play.

I paged through the last turn's battle results once more. It had been a bloodier session than usual, with little of the joking and laughter I normally associated with the game. Maybe we should have gone with something simpler, with lower stakes. Poker, maybe.

Well, it might not last much longer anyway. My domain now had just twelve stars, which was seriously cutting into my production. At least I had managed to take Alpha Centauri last turn, which put me within pouncing distance of Pinky's realm. If I played my moves right, I might recover. I agonized over my orders, typed in a draft, then erased them. I did that a couple of times. I wasn't the only one having trouble, either.

"Are we taking our turns or what?" Peter snapped. He'd submitted his orders long before.

Marta frowned. Peter didn't usually gripe like this. She didn't say anything though, just turned her attention to her *sayar*. A moment later, her green symbol appeared at the top right corner of the game screen on my *sayar*. Fareedh's and Pinky's symbols lit up in quick succession afterward as everyone else finished up their turns.

"Here goes nothing," I said, submitting my turn.

I looked up again as the big three-dimensional star map glowing above the table came to life. Titanic virtual fleets zipped from star to star, and bright and violent flares erupted when opposing forces met. More than the usual number converged on Pinky's red domain. He cried out in surprise with the sound of a dying accordion. What had been a mighty realm shrank under the onslaught of three battle groups, each belonging to a different player. Only Peter hadn't pounced on him.

"I guess I know who *my* friends are," Pinky said. He collapsed like a deflated ball, with matching sound effects.

"Don't take it personally," I said. "You just left yourself open." I leaned back in my chair. I felt kind of deflated, too. I was glad to be back in the game, but I found I wasn't super excited about committing to hours more of play.

"I'm surprised you didn't come after me, Peter." Fareedh pointed out his undefended yellow band of stars bordering Peter's blue domain, itself now down to only eight stars. Peter had been playing quickly, carelessly, most of the game. "Did you forget to put in an attack order?" Fareedh persisted. "If you like, we can reset the turn and call it a free mess up..."

Peter abruptly threw his *sayar* at the table. It bounced and clattered to the floor. I looked at him, speechless.

"Peter—" I began.

"I'm sorry I'm not playing up to your standards. I'll just bow out, okay?"

"You don't have to," Fareedh said, his voice placating. "I'm sorry."

Peter grabbed the edges of the table. "I don't think I'm up for playing tonight." His tone was calm, but there was a brittle edge to it. "Sorry to ruin things. You can divvy up my empire." He got up and left, ignoring Marta's outstretched hand.

A shocked silence remained. The room's air filter chuffed quietly from the corner.

"I should go talk to him," I said, pushing my chair out to stand.

Marta put her hand on my arm. "No, leave him be, he'll be alright." But she didn't sound very sure.

Launch Plus Three (Standard)

The knock on my door came around midday. I found I was happy for the interruption, as I hadn't really talked to anyone since the game had fizzled out the day before. I dropped my *sayar* on the bed and sat up, swinging my legs over the edge and planting my feet on the deck. "Come on in," I called.

The hatch opened. It was Marta, wearing a red sleeveless dress with pink highlights. I hadn't seen this pattern before, and she looked really good.

"Hey, have you got a minute?" she asked. There was something tentative in her tone.

"Sure," I said. "Sorry about the mess." Three days I'd been on *Majera,* and I still hadn't gotten settled. I was still fishing clothes out of suitcases instead of hanging them, and the dirty laundry was in the corner. I hadn't used the Maker to print anything new since I came on board. I'd probably just wear the same old stuff I'd brought with me and run it through the Maker's clean cycle.

Marta came and sat down next to me on the bed. Not that she had a choice, since I hadn't made any chairs. She looked at my *sayar.* "What are you reading?"

"An adventure novel." I tapped through to the title page. *Beyond the First Frontier: A Historical Swashbuckler.* The cover picture had two old spaceships, the kind with the giant engine nozzles in the back and huge bulges in the middle from their ancient Drives, shooting some kind of beam weapons at each other. At ridiculously close range, of course. Nine hundred years of science fiction, and they *still* got space combat wrong.

Marta gave the book a quick glance, then looked around my unfinished room. "You cleared your Exhibit Table," she said, tilting her head at the simple stand on the wall near the head of the bed. Last time she'd seen it, back on Vatan, it had been crammed with stuff. It was nearly bare now, with only a coaster from *Le Frontière.*

"Yep. Not a whole lot to put on it just yet. I'm going to put something from every planet we visit."

She turned to the wall the door was set into and smiled a little bit. "And you still have that picture of Helmi Kader." In the holo, Helmi was staring out over the red sands of Syr Darya, her goggles up on her ruffled blond hair, cape gently streaming. The ruined buildings of a long-dead alien race lay blurred behind her.

"She used to make me so jealous," Marta added with a little laugh. "You'd go on and on about her."

"I remember. You hid my holo for a week once."

"Yeah, well. She was a hard standard to live up to."

"Don't put yourself down," I said, but my answering smile faltered. "I am sorry about that. I could have been more considerate."

"It's water under the bridge," she said, playing with a curly lock of hair. Her expression went serious again and she looked down at the bed for a while, not saying anything.

"Hey," I said. "You all right?"

Marta took a breath, as if composing herself. Then she looked up at me.

"Kitra," she said, "I'm worried about Peter."

"Because of last night?"

She shook her head, earrings jangling softly. "It's more than that. He hasn't been himself since the first day."

"You mean since we Jumped."

"Yeah. When we're together, he just broods. Or he frets and I need to calm him down." Marta tugged at her hair. "It's worrying me. You know Peter. He can be moody sometimes, but this is something more. He's...well, he's terrified. I don't know what to do."

"Hey," I said. "You can always talk to me."

"I know. That's why I'm here." She fiddled with her fingers. "*I'm* scared, too, you know. Sometimes I need someone to tell *me* everything will be alright." She gave me a hopeful look, her eyes shining a little.

I shifted uncomfortably. It wasn't like I could say everything was just fine. I didn't know that. Nobody did. We could be going anywhere, and where we were headed might not be anyplace nice. I didn't know what to say.

"Well," I stammered, "you're welcome to hang out for a while. Um..." I looked around the room, my eyes settling on the pack of cards I'd printed on the first day. "You wanna play Old Maid?" I gave her a broad smile, picking the deck up and waggling them in front of her enticingly. "Just like in the back of French class."

She laughed a little at that. "We got away with so much in that class," she said.

"I think we gave Mr. Leetal all of his gray hairs that year."

"Yeah..." Marta's smile was a fragile thing. "Do you think...could I have a hug first?"

"Oh, yeah! Of course," I said. I could do that, at least.

She wrapped her arms around me and squeezed tight, and I followed suit. My lips cracked into a smile of their own accord. It dawned on me that I'd needed the hug as badly as her. Marta was warm and soft. We stayed like that awhile. It felt good, familiar.

A little too familiar. I felt my body react with a warmth that was both pleasant and unsettling. My heart thudded. I hadn't expected this reaction.

I heard her voice, close to my ear. "Kitra, do you ever miss it? Us, I mean?"

I froze. What could I say to that? Marta and I were best friends, and for a while we'd been…more. No, that wasn't the right word. We'd tried something different, something we both thought we wanted, but which just hadn't worked out. There hadn't been a conscious decision to break up—after a while, it had just been over. Then Peter and Marta had gotten together, and I'd stopped thinking about it at all.

I sure as hell couldn't think about it right now, not under these circumstances. I pressed her away gently.

"Things are different now," I said simply.

She looked down. "I know. You're right. I didn't expect…" she trailed off. She let go of my hands and began to rise.

"Hey, I didn't…I mean, we can still talk," I floundered.

Marta shook her head, a tight smile on her face. "It's all right. Thanks, Kitra. I should go check on Peter." She darted out of my room, leaving me alone. I pushed my hair back, looked down at the floor, and sighed.

This was going to be a long week.

Launch Plus Five (Standard)

It was my turn to make dinner. Pinky offered to help, which is always a mixed blessing, but by this point, I was happy for any company. Marta wasn't talking to me, and for all our years of friendship, I had no idea what to say to make things less awkward between us. Peter spent most of the time holed up in his room. Fareedh had retreated to his *sayar*, double and triple-checking everything. Last night, we hadn't even talked to each other at dinner. Just played with our *sayars*, lost in our own thoughts, and then we had gone back to our rooms. It was funny. Five people cramped into a tiny ship, and I was still lonely.

It was so different from what I remembered of my childhood. Taking giant strides on low gravity worlds. Playing tag under skies that were every color of the rainbow. Even the long periods when we were stuck shipboard were okay because we had school and lots of places to explore on the emissary cruiser. It even had a small park inside.

I'd settled on spaghetti for dinner. It was easy and about the limit of my cooking skills. Pinky was opening the cans and I was reconstituting the pasta. He was whistling from somewhere. Maybe his whole body. I usually like the strange alien tunes he comes up with. This time, though, I found it a little grating.

Mostly, I was just sort of zoning out, brooding. Gradually, I noticed that Pinky had emptied half a container of garlic into the sauce, and there was a big handful of chopped spices in his lumpy fist. His thick fingers slowly uncurled over the simmering pot.

"Hey! What are you doing?" I cried.

"Making up for last night," he said, blithely opening his hand and stirring the mixture with one of his others.

"Um, granted Peter wasn't up to his usual standard, but how are we supposed to eat that?" I looked dubiously at the pot. The sauce had been orange. It was now dark green.

Pinky lowered his head-stump and sniffed. It was purely a dramatic gesture, seeing how he breathes with all of his skin. "Seems okay to me."

I shook my head. "No, we're going to have to add more sauce to make it edible. Which means we'll need to use more supplies." I sighed. "It's just as well. We should have at least *one* real meal on this trip, right?"

Pinky stopped stirring and turned to look at me. His whole body, not just his eyespots. "Something wrong, Kit?"

"Yeah," I said, looking at him. "It'd sure be nice if someone had any clue where we're going." I regretted the words as they came out. It wasn't fair.

"Kit, I can do all the math in the world," Pinky said calmly, "but we could be heading anywhere in a ten light year radius from Vatan. Without stars, I've got nothing to go on."

"I know, I know. It's not just that." I bit my lip. "Marta came looking for reassurances the other night, and I wasn't able to help." I paused, then decided to tell it all. "We hugged. There were feelings."

He raised a couple of palms up, a Pinky shrug. "What else is new?"

I gave him a gentle shove. "I'm serious. Nothing happened, but I think she's embarrassed."

Pinky's rubbery flesh pulsed subtly. "Are you embarrassed?"

"Oh, a little bit. I don't know. Things haven't exactly been normal since we took off."

The alien nodded. "That's right. Things are weird. So people are going to act weird."

"What do I do?" I asked.

"How should I know? But whatever you're doing, it's not working. Try something else." He turned back to the pot. I frowned. Pinky was no help at all. And now he was ignoring me, like everyone else. I glared at him, ready to give him a piece of my mind. His next move stopped me short. He was inching his big fingers toward the garlic again. Slowly. Deliberately. I pushed his pseudopod away from the jar. "What are you doing?" I asked.

"Who, me?" He slithered his pseudopod over my arresting hand like only one of his kind can do, again threatening to put in more garlic.

"Are you *trying* to ruin dinner?"

He didn't answer. Instead, he grabbed some... oh Lord, really? Anise? Why did we even have that on board? Pinky knew I hated the stuff. Now I was fending off two of his pudgy arms. He held the spice jars threateningly above the sauce and started saying, "Oooh! Oooooh! They're gonna fall in!"

Pinky had clearly gone crazy. I grabbed him around the middle and pushed with all my strength. It was like hugging a giant gum eraser, the kind used for art. He let me drag him away from the pot, and I saw his skin tinge brown with amusement.

"You're just messing with me, aren't you?" I accused.

"Am I?" he said drily.

Right. Pinky was doing what he always does. Like when I was six and had scraped my knee, and instead of letting me cry, he'd turned himself into a ball and bounced around me until I was thoroughly distracted, the pain forgotten. I scrunched up my nose and made a face at him.

He wriggled the top of his "head" at me, Pinky's version of a wink,

I guess. I snorted, feeling my lips curving into a smile despite myself. I rubbed Pinky's head affectionately. "All right. Point taken." Then my eyes widened as my freed up mind started working again. *Of course!* We were worrying for nothing. And if I'd spent less time moping and more time thinking, I'd have figured things out a long time ago.

I stood up straight, feeling better than I had since the trip had begun.

"Let's get dinner cooking and everybody together. I've got something to say."

Chapter 7

Looking around the wardroom table, it was hard to believe that this was the same crew that had laughed around the party table just five days before. Peter sat in sullen silence, his unbrushed hair limp over his forehead. Marta looked at him and then me without expression. Fareedh's face was a mask. Only Pinky showed interest, his coarse skin mauve-tinted and restlessly twitching.

Well, there was still time to fix things.

"All right, everybody. Listen up." My tone was sharp, for my benefit as much as everyone else's. I was done being passive. "We've spent the last five days worrying about what's on the other end of this Jump, letting our imaginations run wild and expecting the worst." I paused.

"Well, I know where we're going, and we're going to be okay."

Fareedh raised an eyebrow. That had got his attention. Peter was looking at me now, too.

I went on. "We've been thinking that because we didn't plan this Jump we could be going anywhere. That isn't actually true." I stressed the last four words. "Peter. Based on our hydrogen consumption, how far are we going?"

"Like I said. It's a max-Jump. Around three parsecs, give or take, if we're going anywhere."

"We definitely are," I said. "Fuel consumption doesn't lie. If we were going nowhere, like Pinky suggested, or to somewhere close, we'd have used less fuel when we went into hyperspace. And I'll bet my mother's teacups that the insertion back into normal space, when we use the same amount of fuel going out of Jump, will prove me right."

"How does that help us?" Peter asked. "The odds of us coming out of Jump next to a star, much less an inhabited one, is essentially zero. Space is big."

"Yep. Nevertheless we *are* going to come out near a star," I said triumphantly.

Fareedh was leaning forward now, bony elbows on the table. His dark eyes were fixed on me. "How do you figure?"

"You gave me the clue, Fareedh. You told me that *Majera* Jumped to coordinates that were already in the old Nav system."

"Sure, but I don't know what they are."

"It doesn't matter. We don't have to. Just the fact that they exist is enough."

"I don't follow…" But I saw Fareedh's eyes go unfocused with thought.

I waited a moment, wondering if he'd figure it out. Then I plunged on anyway. "That coordinate library is like the quick-contact on your *sayar*. They're places the ship used to go the most often. Now, it's clear the old Nav system knew where we were coming from because it waited until we were the exact minimum safe distance from Vatan before throwing us into Jump. And wherever we're going, it's got to be a place *Majera* has been before. Otherwise, why set up an automatic routine?"

"Oh!" Marta got it first, her eyes wide. "It'd have to be a place with a port, otherwise why go there so often? So we just need to find which inhabited system is exactly three parsecs from Vatan, and we'll know where we're going. You're brilliant, Kitra!" I felt heat in my cheeks. It was great to see her really smile again.

Pinky held up an overlong finger. "That only gets us half-way. Space is big. And there are, assuming some margin of error since fuel use isn't precisely correlated to distance…" he was silent a moment. "…four settled star systems at a distance of three parsecs from Vatan. One of them is Sennet."

"So we plan for *all* of them," I said. "It still means we're going to be fine." I put my hands on my hips. I was pretty proud of myself.

"Just one thing," Marta noted. "These are old coordinates. The ship's *sayar* was programmed who knows how many years ago. Haven't the stars and planets moved out of place by then?"

I thought a moment. There was always a damned catch.

"*Majera* wasn't retired that long ago," Fareedh said. "The coordinates can't be that old."

"Still, we don't know for sure," Pinky said. "Stars move relatively quickly, even in just a year. They're all in orbit around the galactic center, after all."

Peter cleared his throat. We all looked at him. He looked alive, like he had woken up from a nightmare and realized it wasn't real. "Look, I'm normally the downer here, but I think you're right, Kitra. I think we're going to land bullseye in a system."

Marta smiled and put her hand on Peter's. "Why's that?" she asked.

He turned to face her. His eyes had lost their haunted look. "The system that threw us into Jump was designed to be automatic so you wouldn't have to update coordinates every time you went somewhere. Otherwise, what's the point? It wouldn't Jump us into a planet or a star or something. It's got to keep itself updated as to where all these objects will be at any given time, right?"

I looked at Fareedh. He nodded. "Sure, that makes sense. It's not even that difficult a program. You're probably right."

That's what I needed to hear. I thumped my fist on the table. "All right, then! Here's what I want us to do." I pointed at Pinky. "You call up maps of all the systems we might be going to. Figure out which planets are likely destinations.

"Fareedh, when Pinky's got his coordinates, see if you can use them to crack your code. I bet they'll be a key to understanding how the old Nav system worked."

I turned to Marta. "In the best case scenario, we end up right off Sennet or wherever, and we're done. But if we pop out far away from our destination, we need to be prepared for a long trip in real-space. So no more haphazard meals. Let's make a real plan, count our calories, and eat scientifically. Enough to last however long it takes us to get to port. Call it a week?"

"You got it, boss!"

"And Peter..." He'd sunk the lowest. I wanted to make sure he was the busiest. "For the same reason, you should dig through that junk pile you brought on board. Make a manifest of anything that might be useful. Then run the engine and antigrav through every diagnostic you can think of. Work with Fareedh if you need to. I want to know that our systems will be online and reliable when we leave Jump." He nodded enthusiastically.

"Finally, starting tonight, after we know where we could be going, we're going to run simulations. With the autopilot off, I want us to be able to fly anywhere on the list blindfolded. When we pop out of Jump, we should be ready for anything." I balled my fists and rested them on my hips. "Who's with me?"

The effect was electric. Marta was already half out of her chair. Pinky was bright magenta.

Peter nodded, jaw set. "Let's do this."

Launch Plus Seven (Standard)

"Green light!" Pinky called out triumphantly. He looked up from his panel, formed a big fist and offered it to me. I thumped it with enthusiasm.

I looked through the Window at the simulated starport. The recreation was hyper-real, even down to the little virtual family looking at us from beyond the landing pad, and the sky traffic zooming back and forth amid the high Sennet skyline.

"How did we do, guys?"

Fareedh's voice answered, "Four minutes off optimal for approach, 14.8 seconds off optimal for landing. About as close to perfect as we're going to get."

He was probably right. This was the seventh landing run we'd done for Sennet. It wasn't the flying that was so hard, it was following the complicated Space Traffic Control rules. Or, at least, the ones that came packaged in our simulator. I had to assume they were close to the real thing.

"Marta did the work," I said, giving her a thumbs up. "She handled the communications beautifully. I just had to ride the guidance beams." Marta gave me a grateful smile. "Anyway, it's good we did so well. I don't think there's time for another run." I glanced at the Jump clock display, its numerals counting down one by one. There were only twelve minutes until we left Jump.

"Wow. We *have* cut it close."

I leaned back in my chair, clasped my hands and cracked knuckles. The last two days had been a lot more fun. Our activity had kept us too busy to worry about stupid stuff like dying in the middle of space or overlong hugs.

"So..." Fareedh began, wearing a sly grin. "Who wants to put money on where we're going?"

"You don't think it's going to be Sennet?" Marta asked.

"I'm just saying, there're four options."

I swiveled my chair to face him. "What's your guess?"

"I'm thinking Yavuz," he said.

"You're *hoping* Yavuz," Peter teased.

Fareedh raised his eyebrows and his tone was exaggeratedly hurt. "There's more to Yavuz than the Red Light district, you know."

"Not the way you've described it," Marta giggled. I looked dubiously at Fareedh. I'd missed this conversation. "You've been to Yavuz?" I asked.

He shook his head. "Of course not! Just read about it. Anyway, I'm picking it because it's a good stop for Navy folks wanting some R&R."

Peter stood and stretched his brawny frame, then took a second to straighten his shirt. "As long as it's not St. Helena. It'll take a week just to get fueled at that one-tank base, let alone serviced."

I had to smile. A couple of days ago, we had all been in the dumps, convinced that a dire fate was inevitable. Now we were complaining about being planetside at a small colony for a bit. Honestly, I kind of liked the idea of an unspoiled, half-explored world to play on. Provided I had enough money to rent an air-car that long. My account balance had gotten pretty low, and banks tended to be stingy with credit if you didn't keep funds at their planetary branch, which made sense when every star system was a week away, at minimum.

I caught Marta looking at me. She looked down, then at Peter. Fareedh saw the exchange and gave me a questioning look. I pretended not to notice. It would be good to get off ship for a bit, away from everyone. I needed to put things in perspective and figure out where all of these relationships were going.

"I for one will be happy to breathe fresh air again," Marta said, a touch too lightly, still clearly nervous. "I can't wait until we get out of Jump so we can turn the engines on and get somewhere. Right, Peter?"

"That's a fact." He took her hand and squeezed, and she gave him a little smile. I swiveled back to face the Window. Yeah. A few days off on my own sounded like a great idea.

"Ten minutes," Pinky announced.

Now it was for real. I swallowed. "Let's start running exit checks," I said

"Ship's *sayar* reports nominal function, all components," came Fareedh's report.

"The engines are warm and ready," Peter said. "Assuming we make it out, they should work."

Pinky punched his panel and a real-time projection of the local part of the galaxy came to life in front of the Window. The *Majera's* original position, Vatan, was a blinking dot surrounded by a transparent sphere, three parsecs in radius. Four star systems glowed brightly on the surface of the sphere, all on the coreward side, away from the Frontier. Our destination could be any of them. "Navigation controls are still locked," Pinky said, "but I've got courses plotted for all possibilities. Fast courses. Slow courses. Dinner courses. Golf courses. You name it."

I sighed. "Thanks. Pinky."

"Our air recyclers are working fine, and oxygen and carbon dioxide levels are well within safe limits." Marta said. "Though I wouldn't mind getting them professionally overhauled. It's been getting a bit whiffy despite my efforts."

"Con-flatulations," Fareedh murmured. I put my head in my hands. Yep. Two Pinkies.

I started paging through diagnostic displays, just to double-check. I couldn't find anything wrong. The "Tree" was decked in cheery green lights.

"Hey, do you think the Navy's going to want its Drive back?" Marta wondered aloud.

I barked a short laugh. "They sold it 'as-is.' I'd like to see them try to take it."

"They're lucky we don't sue them for reckless endangerment,"

Peter added.

I felt a rippling that began at my toes and fingers and worked its way inward. My inner ear fluttered. It was entirely different from the feeling of going into Jump. Not exactly pleasant, but less nauseating, at least. I hadn't felt it in almost a decade, but it was entirely familiar.

I heard Peter shift in his chair. "Energy to Drive increasing," he said. A pause, then, "Power usage within normal tolerances."

"Is it supposed to feel like this?" Marta's voice trembled.

I gave her a nod and a smile over my shoulder, both as reassurance and trying to make up for earlier in the week. "It's just fine," I said.

I reached for the controls. They were dry, as if I hadn't spent the last several hours sweating on them. The Jump clock showed less than two minutes to egress. Its numbers counted down, green and luminous.

My eyes were glued to that chronometer, hypnotized, the buzzing in my bones increasing. At some point, I discovered my lips were moving, mouthing out the remaining seconds. *Thirty-four. Thirty-three.* I shook my head to clear it and took one last look around the bridge. Peter's eyes were locked onto his screen, a schematic of the engine glowing in neon orange. Fareedh had that spider-like ship's *sayar* diagram up again. Marta stared anxiously at the blank Window, chewing her lip. Pinky had braced himself three-handedly against his panel.

The buzz became a whine in my ears, slowly sliding up the scale from subaudible to near dog whistle. The clock showed ten seconds remaining. I went back to calling out the time, out loud this time.

"...Four. Three. Two. One."

A brief sensation of falling, and then the Window suddenly flickered to life. I gasped with relief. Stars! Black space crowded with stars! I kept my hands on the controls, ready to thrust the ship away from any obstacles. The whine had faded away. Now, my ears strained for the sound of a collision alarm.

Nothing.

I dared to take a breath. One hurdle down. We were alive in normal space.

"Did we make it?" I asked, half to myself.

"See for yourself," Fareedh said. He got out of his chair, rested a hand on my shoulder, and with the other pointed out the Window at the small full disk of a planet sliding into view. It was fiercely bright against the star-speckled background.

"Woohoo!" Marta squeaked. She jumped up and gave Peter a big hug. "We did it!"

I looked back at the world in the Window, a yellow-tinged circle swaddled with orange clouds. Two moons hung in view behind it, one large and close, the other distant. My smile slowly faded. I tapped the panel, angling the view until I saw the source of the planet's illumination. There were two suns, closely orbiting, one dark orange, the other red. I sat down heavily in my chair, suddenly drained. I looked over at Pinky. He looked up from his panel, met my eyes, and nodded.

"What's wrong?" Fareedh asked.

I swiveled to face him, brows creased. "This isn't one of the systems on our list," I said.

Chapter 8

Pinky returned to his panel without a word, and a schematic of the unknown star system filled the Window. At first, the diagram just included the two closely orbiting suns I'd seen, their round shapes flattened a little by their mutual gravitation. *Majera's* position was a fuzzy circle that gradually shrank to a glowing point as the ship's *sayar* refined our position. A blurry ring appeared around the suns: the automatic sensors had found a planet. It was a giant of a world, tens of millions of kilometers farther out from the suns than us. Little numbers appeared next to it showing that it was twice the mass of Four, but with a very low density. It was probably a ball of hydrogen gas.

We watched in tense silence as the next planet registered, a parched little world far inward. At first, *Majera* didn't even try mapping its crazy orbit, close in around the twin suns. A minute passed, then there was a *ping* and the word "Match" spread across the Window in green letters. The orbits of the two discovered planets resolved into sure paths, and three more rings filled in the gaps. There were five planets in all, with the one we were near being number two. The big one was the third. The ship's *sayar* had figured out where we were.

"Anya and Atya," Fareedh said, reading the names that had popped up next to the two stars.

"I've never heard of them." Peter's voice cracked slightly, and he coughed to clear his throat.

I hadn't either. "Pinky, where *are* we?" I asked.

Little pseudo-fingers played with the panel, and the interstellar map was back, a translucent sphere with a 3-parsec radius centered on Vatan. Our position was a blinking dot just outside the sphere's edge. It was nowhere near any of the four systems we'd marked before. In fact, it was practically opposite them. With almost no systems near us, we were in a kind of star desert.

"Well, you were right on the range of the Jump, at least," Pinky said. "Just not the destination. 50/50's not bad, right?" The cheerful tone sounded forced.

"We must be here for a reason," I muttered, tapping the real-time display back up. I wanted to see the planet we'd popped out next to. The yellow world appeared in the Window again, very bright. Through the few patches not covered with clouds, the surface sparkled dazzlingly. Ice or water, probably the latter. The planet was near enough to the suns for water to be a liquid.

Even without magnification, the planet was as big as my fist. I was willing to bet we were pretty near to the minimum safe Jumping distance from it. That suggested we hadn't come here randomly — this was the planet the old Nav system wanted us to go to, and it had put us in optimum position to land there. *But why hadn't it been on the list?*

"I've looked up 'Anya' and 'Atya' in the ship's *sayar*," I heard Fareedh say.

I turned to look at him, my chest tight.

"And?"

"That planet's called 'Jaiyk.' It's almost all water, a bit smaller than Vatan." He raised his eyebrows and looked at me. "There isn't much else in the entry."

Water planet, I thought. That didn't sound too bad. I had a sudden vision of pristine beaches, beautiful waves, a cool drink in my hand, ice cubes tinkling.

"So, we're not lost, exactly," Peter said, color coming back to his face. "But why would the Nav system send us here?"

"Good question," I replied. "What else can we find out about this place?"

That set Marta to tapping at her station next to Peter. A data square popped up on the Window with a rainbow rectangle of color, purple to red and sliced into vertical strips by black lines: a spectrum of the planet's atmosphere. Underneath it was a list of gases and percentages. Methane was at the top, followed by nitrogen, carbon dioxide, and on down into the tiny fractions. Oxygen wasn't there at all.

"So much for fresh air," Marta said with a sigh. "This must be a young system. There's no life down there, or at least, it's not very far along."

The sand castles and hover-skis in my head disappeared as quickly as they'd come. If this was a barren planet and it wasn't on Pinky's list, then there might not be anybody here — there would be no refined fuel to be had.

"Anything else?" I asked, keeping my voice steady. "Can we use the deep radar unit Peter salvaged?"

Pinky tapped his panel, and a previously dark indicator on The Tree flickered to green life. Space black and star white melted into a featureless gray as *Majera* emitted a spectrum of exotic waves, measuring the echoes. The planet was still there, its disk now dark charcoal with a few bright spots, most no more than pinpoints. Islands, probably. They were all bright yellow except for one that was duller than the rest. "There aren't any continents," Pinky said. "At least not on this side."

I pointed out the odd muted dot. "What's with that one?"

"Let's see..." Pinky zoomed in until Jaiyk filled the screen. The dot grew into a yellow crescent with brown mottling along one shore. The layout was oddly regular. I realized what I was looking at.

"Buildings!" I blurted in relief. "It's a settlement." Buildings meant people. In fact, now that I examined the display further, the telltale open square of a starport was unmistakable. It was a pretty big one, too. Even better.

"I'm sure they've got a fuel depot," I said, then turned to my right. "Marta? You want to contact space traffic control? Let's get clearance and land."

"Sure thing," she said brightly. "I'll find out which channel they're using."

I relaxed into my chair as she began tapping on her *sayar*. My thoughts turned to our immediate issue: getting fuel. Did we have enough cash on hand to buy gas for a return trip? Well, if not, we could always put our deep radar unit in hock or something. I pondered further, trying to calculate a reasonable budget. It slowly dawned on me that Marta wasn't talking on the comms. I turned again. Marta wore a puzzled expression. Peter was looking over at her panel. I couldn't read its display from where I was sitting.

"What's wrong?" I asked.

"There's nothing on any of the standard frequencies," Marta said. "No automatic beacons, no bulletins, nothing. The whole planet is radio-silent."

"That's weird," I said. "You'd think there'd be all kinds of chatter."

"Come to think of it," Pinky said, "we didn't see any space traffic either."

"Hmmm," I said. "Any ships would have shown up when we turned on the deep radar. And Marta'd have detected their transponders."

Peter furrowed his brow and pointed at the settlement in the Window. "I bet that's some super-secret military facility. That's why it's not in our library and why Pinky missed it when he was putting his list together."

"Is there anything on the military channels?" I asked.

"Nuh-uh," Marta shook her head. "I'm not hearing anything on *any* band. There should be something, even if it's just scrambled."

"Well." I swiveled to face the screen. If it was a base, it was a big one. There was a town's worth of buildings, their regular layout clearly pre-planned. A gap of about a kilometer separated the bulk of the settlement from the shoreline. "*Somebody* is down there, or was," I said, "and the old Nav system brought us here for a reason. I say we check it out. Besides…" I thumped the panel. "We're practically out of gas. We don't have a lot of options."

"I don't like it," Peter said. "What if they bust us for trespassing or something?"

"One problem at a time," I said, reaching for the piloting controls.

For a moment, I hesitated. This was going to be my first time really flying *Majera*. Levitating off Denizli didn't count. Plus, I had to conserve as much of our limited hydrogen supply as possible; a simple antigrav drop would waste too much fuel. Could I pull it off? The ship's *sayar* took care of a lot of the flight dynamics, but that just made

Majera flyable — the ship couldn't fly itself.

Well, I wouldn't know what I could do until I tried. I took a deep breath and began our descent.

Breaking orbit was the easy part. Just a quick application of thrust, and *Majera* went into a graceful arc down toward the surface. I planned to end up well short of the island. If the settlement was an active Navy base, I didn't want them to think we were a bomb or something. Minutes went by, the disk of the planet filling our screens. *Majera's* skin temperature spiked as we hit the atmosphere, and I flared the ship a bit to spread the heat better across its surface. Indicators jiggled in the virtual gauges, but as with the liftoff from Denizli, there was no sensation of motion, no feeling in my gut.

The controls were stiff in my hand as we plowed through the upper cloud layer, about 20 kilometers up. The gauges started jittering like crazy and *Majera* began to bank to the left. We must have hit a powerful jet stream. That made sense; Jaiyk had a short day and no land to speak of. The planet would be ruled by giant, global weather patterns. I struggled with the controls to keep the ship on course. I still hadn't turned the thrusters on, to save fuel, so we were entirely in free flight, like when I flew my glider.

It was a rough ride. *Majera* was sluggish compared to a glider and I kept overcompensating, making my attitude indicators tilt scarily. What made it worse was that I was essentially flying blind. There was nothing to see out the Window. The clouds obscured everything. I tried switching to deep radar, but that just showed me where the planet's surface was and no other details. I decided a dirty orange nothingness was better than slate nothingness, so I switched the Window back to visual light.

I breathed a sigh of relief once I finally broke the cloud deck. The cross-winds that had made flying such a chore eased up. Unfortunately, the view didn't improve with the flying. Jaiyk was a gloomy world. Nothing but endless gray waves under a slate curtain. We were still several hundred kilometers from the settlement, so I kicked in the engines at low thrust and kept us level at 300 meters above the ocean. The horizon was utterly featureless, but the map at the corner of the Window showed that our course was accurate.

"Jaiyk Control, this is *Majera* inbound from Vatan," Marta called on the general aviation frequency. "We are low on fuel and request clearance for landing." I heard her repeat the message on several other channels.

There was no answer. It was possible that we were too far away and the bulk of the planet was blocking our comms. Still, the lack of response was ominous. I wasn't sure I bought Peter's secret base theory, but the facility looked intact. Even if the base had been abandoned, there could still be automated defenses. I stiffened in my seat and felt a trickle of sweat creep down my forehead.

"Pinky," I said, "keep an eye out for missiles."

"Aye, aye, Captain." He stretched his "head," extended his eyespots on stalks, and peered at the Window intently.

"I meant use your displays!"

"Ohhh..." He retracted his eyes and popped up a radar display. "What'll you do if they shoot at us?"

I eyed the fuel gauge. It was at 3%; I couldn't afford to waste any on dodging.

"That's a fine question," I said.

Ten minutes passed. Twenty. Still nothing but gray below and above. Then Fareedh called out, "It should be coming into view soon."

Sure enough, on the horizon, a lump of darker gray formed a kind of bridge between the sea and the cloud layer. It quickly grew into a sliver of land dominated by a single volcanic cone whose summit was lost in the clouds. We were coming up the narrow axis of the crescent-shaped island.

Marta tried the comms again as we sailed over the rocky beach. Silence. I decided to risk a pass over the settlement. Our fuel was at less than 2%.

The plains surrounding the central peak were dotted with structures, enough to house thousands of people. There was a blunt regularity to the buildings, that lack of artistic expression, typical with military bases. Now I was really nervous. But as I shot over the base's main avenue, I didn't see a single person or vehicle. The place was eerily empty.

"I'm not getting any power readings or heat sources," Fareedh said. "I don't think anyone's here."

"Can we be sure?" Peter countered. "It's so big."

The fuel gauge began flashing orange. "We're going to find out soon enough. I've got to take her down now." I turned the ship hard about and made a beeline for the landing pad. I had my pick of spots to set *Majera* down—there weren't any other craft parked at the port. I hovered us over the giant flat square and rotated the Window to see directly below.

"It looks intact. I'll park over at the edge so we don't have to walk so far to go exploring."

Landing was the easy part, like landing at any civilized starport. I almost, out of habit, sent a signal to the tower before remembering that there was probably no one there to receive it. We touched down just as the orange fuel light shifted to red.

I wiped sweat from my forehead and ran a hand through my hair. The scene from the Window was not too different from any starport: a flat expanse of landing pad stretching off into the squat cityscape. But the leaden sky and the lack of ships, service vehicles, or traffic gave the place a distinct ghost town impression.

I swiveled to face the crew. "All right. First order of business is to figure out what kind of place this is."

"And the second is to get out of here," Peter replied.

I didn't have a comeback for that. He was probably right.

"I don't think anyone's been here for ages…"

Chapter 9

Majera's airlock was just big enough to hold suits, gear, and two people. I cycled the inner door closed, further cementing that claustrophobic feeling. I patted down my suit, smoothing out the bunches, then helped Fareedh with his. We weren't going into the vacuum of space or anything; in fact, the air pressure outside was only a little below Vatan's. We could probably have gotten away with just wearing respirators and air tanks. But it was just above freezing, at 280 Kelvin, and an unknown world out there. Better safe than sorry. I pulled Fareedh's helmet off the wall and handed it to him. It was mostly a big bubble, but the opaque bits were, like the rest of Fareedh's suit, decorated in swirls of color.

"You really like rainbows, huh?" My voice cracked a little.

Fareedh spread out his hands in a shrug. "Who doesn't like rainbows?" He leaned a bony elbow against the duralloy wall, his helmet in the crook of his other arm. "You sound nervous," he drawled.

"Yeah, well..." I looked away. "Poisonous planet. Creepy abandoned base. If it's really abandoned." I looked back at him. "Aren't *you* nervous?"

His smirk softened into something more genuine. "Not as much as I was last week when my screw-up got us into this mess."

"I told you, it's okay."

He nodded. "I know. Thank you for that." He slid his helmet over his poof of hair and locked it into place. "Anyway, I know you'll get us out of here." His smile widened, and his teeth were very white.

I felt my cheeks flush. I straightened up and grabbed my helmet, pulling it on and sealing it airtight to the suit. Fareedh pulled a pair of oxygen bottles off the shelf, handed one to me, and affixed the other to the back of his helmet. There was a good six hours in each. Plenty for a first reconnaissance.

"You ready for this?" I asked, hand on the outer door switch.

Fareedh flashed me a palm out "ok" sign.

I gave the outer door a quick rap, listening to the hollow, metallic echo as if it might tell me something about the alien world beyond it. I closed my eyes, took a deep breath, and cycled the outer lock.

The whistle of air as the ship reclaimed what was in the airlock quickly faded, the pressure dropping to zero. Then the outer doors slid open, and the gust of the planet's air filling the vacuum nearly knocked us off our feet.

Outside, things looked…normal. Aside from the utter lack of spaceships, this could have been any starport. The buildings looked intact. The suit's chronometer, adjusted for Jaiyk's 20 hour days, told me it was mid-morning, but that was all the evidence I had for what time it was. Dark clouds rushed past overhead, driven by a strong offshore wind, and they completely hid the suns.

Because the starport had the usual layout, I had a good idea where to go next. Every starport has a fuel supply, a giant version of a thermos filled with heavy hydrogen kept cold and compressed into liquid form. As we walked along the edge of the pad, toward the space traffic control tower, I had the feeling we were being watched. I half-expected a loud "SURPRISE!" to come in over the suit radio, and all of the port personnel and vehicles to come out of hiding.

It never happened. Closer to the buildings, the true condition of the port became clear. Some of the tower's windows were off their hinges, swinging freely in the wind. A couple of them were gone entirely. Whatever color the slender walls had been when they were built, they were now a muddy brown with streaks of dirty tan. One of the nearby hangars stood open, its door flat on the ground under a pile of debris. At closer inspection, I saw the pad was in poor shape, too. Hairline cracks spread all over, the result of countless years of expansion in the day and contraction at night.

Still, it was a shock finding what was left of the hydrogen tank. It lay on the pad, a stranded metal whale. It was like an enormous hand had knocked it off its fittings and sent it careening to the ground. A giant crack ran most of the way around its middle. Nothing could be in it.

I started to wonder. Had this destruction happened after the Navy left, or did they leave because this had happened? I considered a darker possibility. Had they left at all? Oh Lord. What if we found bodies? The thought made me shiver.

"So, where else can we find fuel?" Fareedh asked calmly, surveying the ruins. I clamped down hard on my fear. If he wasn't scared, then I could damn well get a grip on myself.

"There must be a refinery near the shore," I said after some thought. "That's how it works on most planets. You build one with easy access to an ocean where you can break down the water into its components for fuel."

"And you think the refinery is going to be in better shape than," he waved his hand in the direction of the discolored control tower, "this?"

"I don't know," I said honestly. "But they're usually pretty rugged buildings. And it's the only lead we've got right now." I wasn't about to give up hope.

I looked off in the direction of the ocean. The bleak cityscape, its buildings featureless and ominous, surrounded us. And we were going to have to walk through that to get to the shore.

Raindrops bounced off the bubble of my helmet with a muted roar but left no streaks. I had a perfectly clear view of where I was walking, which only made the town more creepy. The buildings all had that same stained patina of age and neglect as the starport, looking like ghosts of their former selves. All of their airlocks were closed against Jaiyk's poisonous atmosphere. Nevertheless, as I walked down the settlement's main street, I had the distinct feeling like something might jump out at me from a doorway at any moment. *There's no life on this planet*, I insisted to myself. *There's nobody here.*

"I don't think anyone's been here for ages," Fareedh said as if reading my thoughts, his voice soft in my helmet speakers. He was a reassuring presence nearby, his brightly colored suit a sharp contrast to the monochrome of the cityscape.

The base certainly *looked* deserted. Cornices and signs lay broken on the ground. Electronic storefronts glared blankly at me, many shot through with lightning-streak cracks. There was no way to tell what had been inside. Restaurants? Rec halls? Offices? Or maybe their purpose had been more sinister. Could this have been the site of an experiment gone wrong? Goosebumps prickled all over and I imagined mummified bodies contorted in death agony, ready to spill out of the airlocks if we opened them.

Fareedh tripped over one of the many rocks that lay in the street, bits of building that had broken away over the years, or maybe just stones the wind had brought in after there were no people to clean them up. The gravity was lighter here, and it was taking time for us to adjust. I reached out to steady him. "Thanks," he said, taking my hand. His touch steadied me, too, physically and emotionally. I needed to stop scaring myself.

We walked to the edge of the city, picking our way down the broken avenue. I had expected to see the shore immediately after we reached the last building, but the road went on several hundred more meters before ending in a clump of structures by the beach. They were all on an elevated ridge of dirt and concrete. Beyond them, I made out whitecaps and sprays of water.

"They based themselves pretty far inland," I noted aloud.

Things here were better, now that we were away from the dead town. No more dark hiding places for my imagination to populate with monsters and corpses. It was easier traveling, too. The flat top of the road to the beach was cracked from exposure, same as the landing pad, but there weren't buildings to provide debris, and unlike on a living planet, there were no weeds to truly break things down. I found myself relaxing, and I let go of Fareedh's hand. It was a good time to check up on the other team.

"Hey Marta, Peter," I called into my mic. "You find anything?"

Marta's voice was as clear as Fareedh's though she was at least a kilometer away, "Not yet. There was nothing at the base exchange. I'm going to check the mess hall on the way back. You?"

"We're fine. Just a lot of…" *Don't say dead!* "…abandoned buildings. So, you actually got inside the BX?"

"We did. It was cleaned out."

"No bodies?" I regretted asking as soon as I'd blurted it out.

Marta laughed. "Don't be silly!"

"All right. We'll check in after we find the refinery. Good luck."
"You too!"

We got to the other end of the road, a few abandoned buildings flanking the street. They'd been built extra strong and they looked in better shape than the structures in town, even out here where they were less protected. I stopped at the door of the nearest one, a boxy, characterless structure. The airlock panel was blank. No power. I motioned for Fareedh to join me, and we tugged away in opposite directions. The two panels slid apart with surprisingly little resistance.

We went to the inner door without bothering to close the outer one. We couldn't have made a tight seal by hand, anyway. The interior portal opened easily, too. Nothing spilled out. In fact, there wasn't much inside at all. Just a few discarded pallets and some plastic boxes. It was one big room, dimly lit, probably a warehouse. No oxygen showed up on my helmet display. If there had been breathable air here once, it had long since leaked away. Cloudy daylight dribbled in from the windows ringing the upper walls.

I tried to activate the pallets, but their power supplies were either external or long extinguished. Fareedh found nothing but packing in the boxes. The place was a bust. Disappointing, but also reassuring — a ghost town is a lot less scary than a town with ghosts.

We got back outside, and it felt like the rain was letting up. There were even brighter patches in the clouds, as if the suns might make an appearance after all. A quick glance at the chronometer showed we only had three hours of day left. I looked down the ridge road inspecting the buildings. Most of them looked like the one we'd just left, probably not worth checking out. One of them, bigger than the rest, had giant pipes leading from the structure down to the ocean. *That* was promising.

The suns chose that moment to break through the clouds, their light fully illuminating the area around us for the first time. I got a glimpse of the beach proper and caught my breath. The world had been completely transformed.

The beach wasn't sand. It was made up of stones, vivid with opalescence. The waves that had been dismal gray masses now sprouted rainbows at their crests. It was incredible. My mission forgotten, I ran out to the water's edge, the rocks rolling beneath my feet. The ocean made a pleasant pulsing roar. Finally, something that felt alive! I laughed as the prismatic waves crashed in lazy arcs, threatening to cover my boots.

"Be careful, Kitra," Fareedh's voice rang in my ears, a bit too loud. He was scrambling down toward me.

I gave him a jaunty wave and then looked along the waterline. The difference from the gloominess of before was just incredible. It was hard to believe this place had gotten me so worried. I breathed a sigh of relief and turned to head back.

A brief pink flash amongst the rocks caught my eye.

"Did you see that?" I called out breathlessly.

"What?"

I shaded my eyes from the suns and walked toward where I'd seen the flash, stones crunching underfoot. By the time I'd gotten there, Fareedh was beside me. He followed my gaze, looking down at the rocks that made up the beach.

"What are we looking for?"

"I don't know," I said. "Something pink."

"You could just come back to the ship for that," came a voice over the radio.

I laughed. "Sorry, Pinky," I said, picking my way around in a slow circle. "You feeling left out?"

"Nah. Someone has to hold the fort in case aliens show up." A pause, then, "Oh no! They're here!"

"You don't count!"

"Oh! Whew..."

I pored over the ground, but there was nothing but the bright pebbles. Had I just imagined the flash? Fareedh stopped and kicked at the beach a bit. He got to one knee and rummaged around in the clearing he'd made, grabbing a handful of something. "Hey, is this what you're looking for?" He stood and presented his palm to me.

In it were a dozen roughly faceted stones, like none I'd ever seen before. They were a very deep rose and a little translucent, tiny yellow dots floating in them like stars. There was something about the way they distorted the light that made them seem like portals into another world. I peered into the little swirls, losing myself in them.

"They're beautiful!" I exclaimed.

Fareedh pressed them into my hand. His grin was as wide as mine. We both looked up into each others' eyes at the same moment, and time froze. The orange light fringed his hair with a halo-like glow. His smile softened into something more intimate. I swallowed and felt my lips broadening in response.

And then the mother of all waves slammed into us, impossibly high in the light gravity, knocking us over. Turbulent water submerged and pounded me. My hands clutched at glittering rivers of silt above me, and there was nothing solid below. The wave receded, and I was rolled over a few times before I came to rest, my back wedged into the rocks. I blinked at the bright sky, dazed. Droplets on my helmet beaded and then streamed away. Fareedh was a gangly heap at my feet. I came to my senses and stood quickly, helping Fareedh up. We barely had time to scramble out from the path of the next wave. As it was, it nipped at our heels.

When we were safely out of the wave's reach, I turned around and looked at the ocean. What had been a gentle sea was now a roiling cauldron, several feet closer to the short road than it had been when we'd first gotten to the shore. Well, that explained why they'd built so far from the coasts, and why the shore facilities were so high up. Storms probably drove the waves clear to the warehouses we'd explored, especially during a high tide made by the big, close-in moon.

I patted at my suit. Besides the water, there were streaks of slimy gunk on it. It didn't look like mud, more like what would be at the bottom of a pond. That was worrying. What if some of it had gotten inside? I sniffed the air cautiously. It smelled fine, and my skin felt dry. "Fareedh? You okay?" I asked. He was similarly smeared with the stuff.

"Yep. I'm fine. My suit's fine. You?"

"Yeah. I only injured my pride." I looked at my grimy hands and realized that they were empty. I'd lost the stones. I glared at the angry ocean, debating the idea of going back for more. Caution won out; those waves were enormous.

"What happened?" Peter's voice said, concerned.

"Tide came in."

"Be careful!" Marta chirped.

"Yeah. Thanks." I shook my head and blew out a breath. "By the way, I think there might be life here after all."

"Ooo!" Marta squealed. "Please save me a sample?"

"...Su-ure."

The sun retreated behind a front of clouds, and the scenery again became dismal. The spell was broken. It was time to get back to work. I brushed the remaining water and slime from my suit, scraping a little of the latter into a specimen bottle, and turned back toward the building I'd guessed might be a refinery.

"Come on," I said. "Let's see if the Navy left us anything."

The refinery looked intact, at least from the outside. Getting in wasn't a problem. Like with the warehouse, the doors were unlocked. Once we got in, we found there were no windows, nor did the lights work. All we could see was what our suit lamps illuminated, circles of brightness in a lot of dark. I couldn't make much of all the pipes and encasements and other bits; none of them matched my shaky understanding of what distillation machinery should look like. A little of my fear returned. I was no engineer. Maybe I should have gone on the food and supplies patrol. Fareedh could have gone with Peter.

On the other hand, there had been considerations beyond the practical in play. It was good for Marta and Peter to get some time alone together off the ship. Maybe that's why she was so cheerful now. And, well, I'd been avoiding being alone with Marta since the day she'd visited my room. It wasn't that I didn't trust her, exactly. Maybe I didn't quite trust myself. It was frustrating. Intellectually, I knew why we'd broken up. It just hadn't been the right fit. But after the day we'd hugged, every so often, I'd get a flashes of memory: Marta with her cute dresses, jokes we'd shared, her smile...

I shook my head and blew out my breath through wobbling lips in a wet raspberry.

"You alright?" *She's gone crazy*, Fareedh's tone seemed to say. Well, maybe I had, a little.

"Yeah. Just clearing cobwebs," I said.

Fareedh idly clanged one of the pipes lining the concrete corridor as we walked. It echoed with a hollow sound.

"What are we looking for, exactly?" he asked.

"Either the catalytic chamber or the electrolysis chamber," I said, picking my steps carefully through the rubbish.

Fareedh spread his arms. "I have only a vague concept of what those are."

"Oh! Sorry..." I paused, composing my thoughts. "If you shoot enough electricity into water, it breaks down into its atoms, two hydrogens and one oxygen. Hydrogen's what you want for fuel because you can compress it," I clasped my palms together and squeezed, "and fuse it into helium. That's how stars work, and also our engine. With me so far?"

He nodded. I went on, "The thing is, a star can use plain old hydrogen just fine because a star is huge and has lots of gravity to squeeze it. For a small engine, you need a heavy kind of hydrogen, one that fuses more easily. Luckily, any batch of hydrogen has actually got small amounts of heavy hydrogen mixed in."

"So you filter the heavy stuff from the regular stuff."

"Exactly," I said. "Electrolysis for breaking down the water, catalysis for filtering the deuterium and tritium fuel out of the hydrogen." I smiled. When Fareedh talked about *sayar* stuff, he always seemed to know everything. It felt good to be able to explain something to *him*.

We walked a bit further down the corridor. Up far ahead, I thought I saw a sliver of light running parallel to the floor. I motioned for Fareedh to kill his light while I did the same, plunging the hall into darkness. Fareedh put his hand on my shoulder, though I couldn't tell whether he was reassuring me or steadying himself.

I could definitely see the light now. It lit a tiny section of the floor ahead, as if streaming from behind a closed door. My hopes rose. Light meant power...maybe the place was still operational! I switched my light back on and grabbed Fareedh's hand. We loped down the hallway, our footsteps loud in the enclosed space. Sure enough, the corridor ended at a door. I grabbed the handle, pulled, and squinted as bright light assailed my eyes.

I took a step inside, my boot splashing down. The floor was slick with water. Then I saw where the light was coming from. A big chunk of the building's roof had collapsed. Muted light from a cloudy sky poured in, illuminating a place in ruin.

"Well, crap," I muttered.

"It doesn't look so good, does it?" Fareedh echoed.

It looked lousy. On the one hand, this had clearly once been where fuel was processed, with tanks, pumping machinery and other heavy equipment I'd expected to find in a refinery. But none of it looked usable. Duralloy doesn't rust, but plastic fittings erode. There were the remains of offices flanking the area, their plastic walls half-collapsed and wrecked by exposure to sun, water, and wind.

"This place must have been abandoned for decades," Fareedh mused. "I'd say centuries, but then it wouldn't have been in the Nav system."

"You saw the big storms from orbit. I bet hurricanes hit this place all the time," I said. "Things probably started to fall apart pretty quickly after the Navy pulled out."

Fareedh leaned back against a thick pipe suspended horizontally above the floor. "Why do you think the Navy built this giant place only to up and abandon it all?"

It was nice to take a break. I didn't see any promising places to sit amidst all the water and garbage, so I joined Fareedh a few feet down the pipe. "Well," I said, considering. "I don't think the place was attacked. There's no damage anywhere other than what weather might do. And no bodies."

"Who'd attack it anyway?" Fareedh asked, his tone rhetorical. "The last Civil War was centuries ago, and the war front against the Grilchies is on the other side of the Empire."

"Pirates?" I asked, then answered my own question, "No, this base is too big to be a target."

I reached around and rubbed at my back, wishing for the umpteenth time that I could scratch an itch through my suit. I settled for wriggling, which helped some, and thought some more. The Navy people hadn't been driven away. They hadn't unleashed some horror or been wiped out by disease. They hadn't even hurried in their leaving, or they'd have left more behind. That left just one conclusion, the least frightening one.

After all, I'd seen bases disappear before, points of call that the emissary ship stopped visiting. Military installations come and go, according to the whim and budgets of the Empire or the Province. Sometimes, a base might be converted into a civilian city, but there was no reason for that to happen on Jaiyk. No oxygen. No useful life.

Bad weather.

"I think they were just *done*," I said at last.

"Why even build here at all, then?" Fareedh asked. "What's the point of establishing a base in the middle of nowhere?"

It was a good question, and I didn't have an immediate answer. Then the star map Pinky had called up after we came out of Jump came to mind. A pair of suns in a barren region of space. Everything fell into place.

"It's simple," I said, as if I'd known all along. "This region is empty in terms of systems except for this one. No stars for light years around. Jaiyk must have been a way-station, back when our Type 3 was state of the art. The Type 4 was developed around eighty years ago, with almost half-again the Jump range. I bet the Navy just didn't need this place anymore."

"This was a way-station to where, I wonder," he said.

I shrugged, happy to have found a solution to the riddle that didn't involve aliens, zombies, or plagues. "Who knows? It probably doesn't even matter anymore. Things change a lot in eighty years."

He chuckled. "Where's your sense of adventure, Kitra?"

I snorted. "Like I say, one thing at a time. We don't even know if we can get off this sponge of a planet yet, much less find the next one over." I got up and waved for Fareedh to join me. "Come on. Break's over."

The light seemed a little dimmer. We probably only had about an hour of good daylight left, so we needed to prioritize our survey. The three big tanks appeared to be intact and were the most promising. Two of them had big pipes and cylinders running between them and the walls. They had to be part of the catalytic or electrolytic process—but which one? I walked around them with a sinking feeling. Glib explanations to Fareedh aside, I really didn't know what I was looking for. Peter would probably have to come out here tomorrow after all.

I grimly turned my attention to the third tank, a big gray thing with just one pipe going to it. It was just as incomprehensible as the other two tanks. There were words stenciled on this one though, faded beyond legibility. I walked up to the tank and saw that it was covered with years of grime and moisture. I started rubbing at it, and the letters became clearer. A few minutes of effort later, the words were revealed. They said "*Döteryum Depolama.*"

"Ooo!"

"Found something?" Fareedh came over to my side.

"Let's not get our hopes up yet," I said. "It's a Deuterium tank. But I don't know how we'll find out whether there's anything in it." I pointed to what looked like a *sayar* panel on its side. "That thing is long dead."

Fareedh gave the panel a quick look and nodded. He walked around behind the tank out of sight.

"Kitra, you might appreciate this," he called out, tone mild.

I joined him and saw him grinning broadly, pointing at the tank. Out of the other side of the tank jutted a fixture where someone could hook up a hose or a pipe. Sticking up from it was a little round display. It was an *analog* thing, with lines and numbers going one to a hundred inscribed around the perimeter. There was also a red arrow, pointing somewhere around 90.

A smile creased my face as I realized what that meant. It's amazing how quickly a situation can turn for the better.

Chapter 10

Like the trip out, the trip back to the ship was also gray and miserable. A harsh wind from the sea tugged at our suits. This time around, though, I had a spring in my step, not just thanks to the low gravity. We had fuel!

As if echoing my cheerful mood, when we reached the set of starport buildings that ringed the pad's edge, a quirk of the cloud layer created a hole, and brilliant light flooded in through the cityscape. It was at a low angle, casting jagged shadows far along the empty pad. The big sun was already under the horizon, the smaller one just sinking behind the city buildings beyond the starport.

The combination of the clouds and the redness of the remaining sun looked like a witch's cauldron, its contents vivid crimson and in restless boiling motion. I'd never seen a sunset like this before. I made sure to catch some holos of it with my *sayar*, but I doubted that a recording would do it justice. It just went to show that any planet can be beautiful, no matter how hostile.

The ship was a stark silhouette by the time we got there. We cycled through the airlock, went through decontamination (I was *not* going to take chances with the slime), and shucked off our suits. A wonderful riot of smells greeted us. Someone was cooking, real cooking, not just using the Maker. I picked out the savory smell of baked meat, the tang of cabbage, and the sweetness of…apple pie? Fareedh and I looked at each other, goggle-eyed. Then we raced each other down the lower corridor, up the stairs, and into the wardroom.

I think Heaven must look a bit like what we saw. The table was set formally, down to the two extra forks I'm never quite sure what I'm supposed to do with. In the center was a huge, steaming casserole of cabbage, minced meat, rice and, Lord help me, real Lingonberry jam. Pinky was just laying down the last cloth napkin, and he was wearing a ridiculously tall white hat with a poofy top. Marta was there, too, in front of the oven. She turned to smile at me, her face adorably smudged with flour.

"Welcome back!" she said.

I gave Marta a brief smile, and then looked at Pinky in disbelief. "Is that a mushroom sprouting from your head?"

The alien rolled eyespots to Marta, then back at me. "It's a chef's hat, Kitra," he said with exaggerated condescension. "Hats are very important, you know."

Looking back at the table, I shook my head in wonder at the spread. There was a big bowl with slabs of gently steaming flatbread. Next to it was a covered pot of what I guessed was pea soup, judging from the color.

"Marta," I said, "this is a ton of food! This must be half our reserves."

"Oh, no. Actually, you can stretch things pretty far if you're creative. Plus, we found a couple of things on the way back to the ship." She raised her voice, green eyes twinkling. "Peter? You want to bring in what we found?"

I heard Peter's muffled acknowledgment from somewhere in the ship, followed by a grunt and a set of increasingly loud footsteps. When he appeared, he was hefting a giant cream-colored bag over his shoulder. I was impressed. It was a heavy load, even with the lower gravity. He set the bag down by Marta with a grunt. "Fifty kilos of wheat flour," he said, wearing a pleased expression. "There was more, but they'd decayed too far to even run through the Maker." He pointed to the items on top of the retractable shelves above the oven. "We also got that big pouch of dried milk and a couple of cans of honey that look undamaged."

"This stuff plus what we have in stores should last us two more weeks, no problem!" Marta said.

Peter eyed the flour sack doubtfully. "We'll be eating a lot of bread," he said.

"Wait and see," Marta said, unfazed. "I've got a couple of ideas."

"That was awfully kind of them to leave all these goodies for us,"

Fareedh observed.

Peter shrugged. "We had to dig a bit to find these. I don't think they left all that much, and like I said, most of it was spoiled. This is vintage stuff."

I squeezed past the chairs to take a look. The dates were in standard notation. One of the cans of nuts had an expiration date of 2776. I did a quick calculation in my head, converting Vatan's calendar to standard. "Oh, wow. Uh, we're going to take a chance on seventy year old food?"

"Why not?" Marta said, dusting her hands on her apron. "I once ate a piece of a century-old fruitcake. So long as the food is preserved, it should be fine." I raised my eyebrows but said nothing, trusting her expertise.

"I guess that tells us how long the base has been abandoned," Pinky said.

I nodded. "Yeah. That ties perfectly with what I was thinking." I saw Peter cock his head curiously at that. "I was figuring that this planet hasn't got much going for it except for its location," I explained. "When Type 3 was the best the Navy had, they used the base to leap-frog to the other end of the frontier. Jaiyk was the only usable world in the star desert."

"Of course!" Peter cut in, his tone excited. "It all ties together. The Navy didn't bother to remove the old Jump drive from *Majera* because it's old technology, so we got it as a bonus. *Majera* was a scout, so it's no wonder its main destination would be Jaiyk, the one stepping stone across the star desert. That's what was in the old Nav system's memory, and that's why we're here." He looked relieved to know the ship wasn't haunted.

"And now that we're here," Pinky said, "perhaps you should all dig in to this feast we've prepared, hmmm?" He angled his head forward, his ridiculous hat nearly falling off. We all took seats at the table, and I rubbed my hands together eagerly. I felt really at ease for the first time in eight days. We knew where we were and why, the ship was in good shape, and we had supplies. Tomorrow, Peter would go out to the refinery and figure out how to get the gas on *Majera*. And then we could go home.

Launch Plus Eight (Standard)

"It's not enough," Peter said.

I sat down heavily on one of the two chairs folded out from the wall of the "shop." Peter had essentially taken over the room, with electronic odds and ends spread out on several tables. Even his workout equipment was here.

I swallowed, my throat dry.

"I checked it three times," he went on, his tone angry. "We're at 25%. Maybe that's enough fuel for a short Jump, but no way are we making it all the way home."

"We can't stop somewhere along the way?" I knew the answer even as I asked.

"A couple of light years doesn't do us any good!" His voice was nearly a shout. "There aren't any useful stars inside that range."

"Could we get the refinery back online?" I asked.

Peter barked a short laugh. "Are you kidding? It's a shambles."

"What about distilling our own fuel?"

"Yeah, we could do that." His tone suggested the opposite.

"Well, why don't we?"

He glared at me. "If we had our own distilling unit, we could filter and electrolyze the ocean water for fuel. But we don't *have* a unit."

And I should have gotten one before we left. That's what he was saying. He wasn't wrong. But distiller units aren't cheap, and I'd thought we'd be buying our fuel, not having to make it from scratch. Still… "*You're* a genius, Peter," I said, trying to keep my voice level. His anger was catching. "Can't you make one?"

His cheeks flushed as he opened his mouth to snap back a retort. Then he paused, his eyes lighting on my hands clenched into fists. He exhaled and turned. "Of course I could," he said, his voice now more weary than mad. "We've got the parts, between ship's stores and what's left at the base."

"Well then…?"

"It'd take too long. A few weeks to assemble the parts, several days to refine the fuel. Maybe more. That slime you found? Bacteria of some kind. Marta says it's not dangerous, but it's one extra complication."

"But we could still try! We could go on half rations. Maybe find more food in the city."

He shook his head. "We checked the likely spots. You saw what we found. Plus, it's not just the time to make the thing. There's also the trip home."

I put my palm to my forehead. I could feel my pulse throbbing at my temples. "We can't just give up, Peter. If this is our only option, we've got to pursue it."

There was a pause. Peter seemed to be wrestling with something. Finally, he looked at me and said, "It's not."

I stared at him. "What do you mean?"

Again, he hesitated. "I mean, there's another way to get fuel into the ship."

"Oh!" I stood up. "For Lord's sake, why didn't you lead with that?"

"Because it's a bad option."

I put my hands on my hips and waited, our eyes locked. He broke contact first, reluctantly pulling out his *sayar* and showing me a schematic of *Majera*. The fuel tanks were illuminated in orange as well as two passages that went through the ship: parallel lines that started in the tail, went through the wings, and ended in the nose.

"What am I looking at?" I asked.

Peter pointed at the openings in the bow in the diagram. "These are inlets. You open up the hatches, and air can go into the ship as you fly through it."

"How does this get us fuel?"

"See how the lines go along the outside of the tanks? When you fly at hypersonic speed, air goes into them and they hit these magnetic filters." He illustrated with his fingers as he spoke, and his tone became more comfortable, less anxious. "They sort the gasses by density. Most of them—helium, nitrogen, oxygen, methane, whatever—get trapped and shunted back out the back. Hydrogen is the lightest element, and it goes on through the pipe to the aft vent. There, it goes through a similar cycle, with deuterium and tritium ending up in the fuel tanks and the normal hydrogen discarded. It's all one piece, part of the structure of the ship itself. That's why the Navy left it in."

"The atmosphere here has hardly any hydrogen," I said. "We'd never be able to fill our tanks."

"Right." He folded his arms. "This only works if you're flying in an atmosphere that's mostly hydrogen."

"Where are we going to find pure hydrogen to fly the ship through...oh." There was a ball of it nearby, a tremendous world of it. "You're saying we'd have to dive into the heart of that gas giant to get our fuel."

He shook his head. "No. I'm saying *you'd* have to dive into that gas giant. You're the only one who can pilot *Majera*." Peter's expression was bleak, the shadows starkly outlined under his strong cheekbones. "I told you it's not a good option."

I rubbed the fingers of my right hand together, feeling sick. It's amazing how quickly things can turn for the worse.

I sat in my Cleaner, head in my hands, the warm gusts of moisture swirling around me. My thoughts swirled, too. I had a decision to make, and all of our lives depended on it. I frowned, rubbing my raisined fingers together. *All right. Let's review the options one more time.*

Let's say I told Peter to build the distilling unit. We had two weeks of food. Maybe that much air, too. We could ration food but we couldn't ration air, but air was the lesser of the problems. Peter would have to build the electrolysis part of his machine first. He could crack the ocean water into hydrogen and oxygen, and the latter would keep us alive. It was still an open question how long it would take to build the thing, though, or if he even could.

Food was the real sticking point. All right, so we'd go to half rations, which would give us four weeks. I rubbed at the stubborn roll in my stomach. Well *I* could probably weather a period of small or missing meals. But could Fareedh? Or Pinky, for that matter? If it took two weeks to start generating air, another week to begin making fuel, yet another week to finish fueling. Four weeks. Then there was the trip home. Another week.

It all came down to timing. If all went perfectly, we'd just make it. We'd pop out next to Vatan, exhausted and starving, but alive. But there was no margin for error. If Peter couldn't make air in time, or if it took too long to fuel up...

My imagination took over: Fareedh collapsed in his chair, barely more than a skeleton. Pinky gray and pebble-skinned from malnourishment. Marta and Peter blue from asphyxiation. I knuckled my eyes, shaking my head.

All right. How about the other option? Plunging the ship I'd flown just once into a giant planet filled with hurricane-force winds, columns of turbulence, and Lord knows what else. My traitor mind supplied more graphic images: *Majera* on fire. Our spacecraft a cinder, tumbling away from the giant planet. My crew burned to embers. I flinched. No, even the slim chance of survival afforded by Peter's plan to build a portable refinery was better than the certain death we'd face if I tried to skim fuel out of a gas giant.

I blinked and found myself staring at the opaque walls of the Cleaner, blurred by banks of mist. That was it, then. It had to be the first option, bad as it was. I'd towel off, tell Peter to get to work, and we'd do what we could to survive. Hell, this mess was my fault; Fareedh and Pinky could eat my share. I stood, reached to switch off the steam, then paused in mid-stretch.

The argument *hadn't* been decided. My balled fists told me that. There were still two choices. I punched the Cleaner off with a vicious blow. The walls retracted, and cool air rushed in, goosepimpling the hair on my arms and legs into fuzz. The shock of transition helped, clearing my head.

Of course the second option wasn't off the table. I was a pilot, wasn't I? Hadn't I flown hundreds of hours in a glider? I'd made it through some pretty hard weather, buffeted by high winds and thermals. There were times when I'd been up for hours, blown far off course, groping for favorable winds to bring me back home. If I could manage that with just a few hundred pounds of flexi-plastic between me and the air, surely I could do it with 200 tons of shielded duralloy.

I picked a towel up from one of the boxes still littering my stateroom floor and ran it over my hair, tousling it dry. Doubts still gnawed at me. I'd flown my glider long enough for it to feel like a part of me. Its wings were my wings. *Majera* was something else entirely, its stubby winged shape less albatross and more penguin. And instead of soaring on winds, I was going to be plowing right through them at many times the speed of sound. I paused in mid-towel, fear threatening to boil up inside me again.

No. I could do this. I just needed to learn how. It was a matter of experience. Since I lacked experience flying *Majera*, I was just going to have to get some. My eyebrows shot up as a thought came to me. I knew how to get that experience. Plenty of it.

My *sayar* was on the nearly empty Exhibit Table. I strode over and thumbed Fareedh's contact. He picked up almost immediately. Then his eyes widened in surprise.

"Uh…" he stammered.

I stabbed the audio-only button and felt heat rising in my cheeks. Whoops.

"Hey, Fareedh," I blurted, my voice squeaking only a little. "Has Peter told you about our fueling options?" Well, hey, I wasn't sure how I was going to start this conversation, and now we'd fast-forwarded things to the meat of it.

He recovered his composure admirably. At least, *his* voice didn't squeak. "Yeah, a few minutes ago. He said we either try distilling fuel here or we scoop the third planet. He didn't seem enthusiastic about either option."

"Yeah. Neither am I." I took a deep breath, then plunged on. "But if I have to choose, I'm leaning toward the second. There's not enough food, and I don't think you can skip a meal, let alone a week's worth."

I heard the smile in his voice. "Hey, now. No need to get personal."

I wrapped my towel around me and toggled the *sayar* back to visual mode. "I'm serious. I don't want to lose a gamble and then watch us all starve to death or suffocate. If we've got two low-chance options, I'd rather take the quick one. Especially if it's the one I have more control over."

Fareedh looked at me seriously, his eyes large and dark. He nodded slowly. "I get it. What can I do to help?"

I took a deep breath through my nose, exhaled. "Do you think you could use the ship's *sayar* and program a model of the upper layers of the third planet's atmosphere?" I asked. "For a simulation, I mean. If I'm going to pilot *Majera* through it, I want as much practice as I can get."

He rubbed at the dark stubble on his chin, considering. "Yes, I should be able to do that. My freshman project was something like that, actually. We were making climate models of Four."

"It doesn't even have to be super accurate," I said. "Heck, it's probably not much different from the flying we did over Jaiyk, right?"

"You'd be surprised," he said, leaning forward. "The air pressure might be the same at the altitude you plan to fly, but all that gas makes for chaotic conditions." He looked levelly at me. "Even so, I believe you can do it. I'll be happy to code the simulation."

I sat down and wiped away the last drops on my forehead with the back of my hand.

"Thanks, Fareedh. I knew I could count on you."

He smiled, then swept his eyes over me and winked. "Of course."

I snorted and looked away, but I was smiling too.

"It basically comes down to one question, doesn't it?" Pinky sprawled in his wardroom chair, looking as close to human as he gets. Two almost-arms, two almost-legs, shorter and thicker around than me. He looked over at Peter, then at me. "Which of you has more confidence in themselves?"

Marta wrinkled her nose at that. "Oh come on, Pinky. There's a lot more to it than that. You heard Kitra! There's timing, there's the chance of finding parts for Peter's unit, all sorts of things to consider."

The alien raised an overlong finger and waggled it in front of where a nose would have been on a human. Then he pointed it at Peter. "How sure are you that you can find what you need to make the electrolysis machine *and* the heavy hydrogen filter?"

"I don't know. Pretty sure, I guess," Peter said, sounding not at all sure. "I'd need to find a chamber big enough to process enough water at a time. There's got to be something somewhere. The filter's, uh, a little trickier."

"And you think you could get this done in three weeks?" Fareedh asked.

"Maybe." Peter sat up in his chair. "Probably. I've already drawn up the schematics."

Pinky pointed his other hand at me. "Kitra, how sure are you that you can pilot *Majera* through a gas giant?"

"I can do it," I said with more confidence than I felt. "With Fareedh's help."

"I saw how you struggled flying the ship when we got here, and that was just thirty minutes on a terrestrial world," Peter retorted. "You really think you would last for hours in that ball of hell? I'm sorry I even brought the idea up." He looked angry, frustrated—with himself or me, I couldn't tell. Maybe both.

"Why are we rushing to make this decision?" Marta asked, patting Peter's arm. "Couldn't Peter start working on his device, and if it doesn't work out, *then* we go to the third planet?" He looked up at her and nodded in agreement.

Fareedh drummed on the table with his right hand, considering. "I don't think we have the time. It's something we have to stay on Jaiyk to finish since the parts, if they exist, are here. If we get a week down the road, and then it turns out Peter can't build the thing, that's half our air supply gone. We have to commit to something soon."

Pinky folded his arms over his round middle and rolled his eyespots to me. I glanced away. My gaze came to rest on the clock on the wall, probably the most important instrument in the ship right now. The seconds flashed away, one by one, counting down what could be the last remaining moments of our lives.

"Fareedh's right," I said abruptly, standing up. "Let's put it to a vote and be done with it. All those in favor of diving the gas giant for fuel, raise your hands." I put my palm in the air. Pinky and Fareedh followed suit without hesitation. Marta looked at Peter, then at me. Her lips were pressed together tightly, and she stared at me, assessing, as if she was searching for something behind my eyes.

Then she raised her hand. "If Kitra says she can do it, I know she can," she said, a little smile appearing at the end.

I caught Peter's flash of anger out of the corner of my eye, but by the time I was looking directly at him, it had already disappeared. He returned my gaze with flat eyes.

"I guess that's it, then," he said. "It's decided."

Chapter 11

Launch Plus Ten (Standard)

White billowy clouds streamed in the Window. I gripped the stiff controls, my knuckles white. Air pressure was already 300 kilopascals, more than twice as high as Vatan's at sea level, and rising. The altimeter read…well, it didn't read at all. Where does the surface even begin on a gas giant? They don't have a solid bottom. Just thicker and thicker layers of hydrogen mixed with some helium until the density is so great, it's not flying anymore, it's swimming. Oh, sure, way down below the hydrogen ocean, there might be a rocky core, but I'd never see it personally. No ship could make it even a quarter of the way before being crushed.

I struggled with the controls. It's one thing to drive on the surface of a planet. It's another to fly over one. It's a third thing to soar *into* a planet. The yaw and bank indicators told me I was doing something wrong, that the ship wasn't flying straight or level. The lines in the virtual gauges bobbed and rolled like the horizon of a stormy sea. Every time the ship tilted out of alignment, yellow lights flashed and the hull temperature rose as winds blasted the ship's skin. *Majera* steered like a whale, and I had a tendency to over-control. Unlike flying a glider, there was no visceral feedback. The ship could do cartwheels but the antigrav would keep us completely still. That kept me from falling out of my seat, but also made it difficult for me to connect with the ship.

"I just can't get the *hang* of this!" I said, then flinched. It sounded whiny, even to my ears.

"You're doing fine, Kitra," Pinky said. "Hang in there."

"Fuel tanks up to 12%," Peter called out crisply.

I felt my stomach clench, and cold flowered in my chest. I looked at the chronometer. I'd only been at this for twenty minutes, and I was already exhausted. I made a quick mental calculation to see how much longer I had to keep going, and that made it worse. There was no way I could keep this up for another three hours. I gritted my teeth, trying to focus, but those damned gauge lines kept getting away from me. It was like trying to stand on a teeter-totter. The moment you got out of balance, the whole thing tipped and you were gone.

Okay. Deep breath. You can do this.

I willed my hands to steady, only making the tiniest of movements. I tried to anticipate the rolls, the pitches, the yaws before they happened so they wouldn't get out of control. Throbbing aches grew in my shoulders. I hadn't realized how much effort went into staying stock still. The effort seemed to pay off, though. One minute went by. Another. I was doing it; our flight path was steady. I relaxed a little and flexed my fingers, the sweat-absorbent material of the controls not quite up to the job I was giving them.

My respite lasted exactly three seconds. An alarm bell went off, and I went tense again. A red-framed pop-up appeared in the Window telling me that local wind speeds were up and climbing rapidly. I hoped that I'd just found a small jet stream and tried angling away, gently. But there was no escaping it. Wind speeds jumped again, and with it, turbulence. I saw the gauge lines bounce and jerk.

Any spinning planet creates cyclonic storms, call them *kasirga* or *taifun* or hurricane. On a gas giant, hurricanes are storms several times the size of Vatan. They take hours to sail through, and you don't always see them coming. Now I was trapped in one, being bounced around like a toy in a bathtub. My roll gauge showed I was banking hard to the left, the wingtip arcing to point downward. I pushed my stick to the right to level off, but *Majera's* aft started to pivot clockwise. I tugged at the rudders to compensate. More red pop-ups. The ship began to tumble. *Majera* was being pummeled by winds in places that were never supposed to be exposed to direct pressure.

A loud klaxon went off. Hull temperature was reaching a critical level. The streams of clouds in the Window flew by in random directions as *Majera* spun end over end. I jerked at the controls, though they might as well not have been attached to anything for all the good they did. We were entirely at the mercy of the hurricane, flung into the depths of the planet.

The Window went black and the flight sticks went limp in my hands. I looked up, hating what I was going to see. "MAJERA DESTROYED" appeared on the screen.

I'd failed again.

I had laughed the first time I'd flunked the simulated run. *Just rusty*, I'd thought. The second time, I'd cursed up such a streak even Fareedh blushed. But now…I felt the tears coming, and a lump in my throat. Three runs, and I wasn't any closer to mastering the flight. I had to face facts. There was just no way I could keep this up for the several hours a fuel dive would take.

I stared at my panel. The gauges were frozen in their last crazy positions. I couldn't turn to face my crew, especially not Peter. I knew what his expression, the anger in his eyes would say. And he was right.

We're all going to die, and it's Kitra's fault.

I tried the simulation a half dozen more times. All were failures. Peter couldn't watch me after a while and left without a word; I didn't know until I stopped hearing his reports. The others stuck with me longer. They didn't really bail on me—Pinky chased them out. He knew that look on my face, that I was going to scream at the next person who talked to me. After the last run, I just sat in my pilot's chair for a long time, staring at the stars out the Window. They were stationary, as if *Majera* wasn't moving at all. Only the slowly growing disk of the third planet, not quite directly in front of us but at the end of our curving trajectory, betrayed our speed. I looked for comfort in the constellations, as I often had back home, but they were distorted by our distance from Vatan. They looked alien, like something out of a nightmare.

The stars became blurry, obscured by tears. I couldn't fight it anymore. Lord, I hate crying. It's what you do when you're out of options. It reminds me of earlier times, bad times when I'd woken up from nightmares, calling for my mother, realizing all over again that she could not ever comfort me again. She couldn't help me now, either.

So I cried, and I hated myself for the weakness. At least no one could see me.

I was so wrapped up in myself that it must have been at least five minutes before I realized that Pinky was sitting in his chair next to me. I jumped in my seat, my last sob turning into an undignified snort. "Pinky, when did you get here?"

He eyed me, his inhuman spots betraying no emotion. "I've *always* been here. But if you mean this particular spot, just a moment ago."

I wiped my eyes. "I don't understand how you can sneak around so quietly, as clumsy as you are," I said. At least my voice was under control.

He tapped his naked pseudo-feet. "Rubber-soled shoes," he said. "Everyone's gone to bed. What are you doing in here?"

"Feeling sorry for myself," I said honestly, brushing my hair back. "And feeling awful for the position I've put you all in." I never could hold much back from Pinky. Maybe it was because he was an alien. I never felt like he judged me.

"We volunteered to be here," he said, folding two of his three arms.

"Sure you did," I said skeptically. "No, Peter was right. I'm always dragging you into stuff."

"That's silly. You never laid a hand on us."

I rolled my eyes. "C'mon, Pinky. You know what I mean."

"I do," he nodded. "And again, 'That's silly.' We all came willingly. If you had to convince any of us first, that just means you had good arguments."

"Well, if I hadn't convinced you with my so-called wonderful arguments, we wouldn't be here."

"What's wrong with here?" he asked blandly.

Was he being deliberately stupid or was he just trying to aggravate me? "Pinky, we're ten light years from anywhere, and we're probably going to die," I said in a rush, not bothering to keep my voice down. "I've been practicing that stupid simulation all day, and I keep failing."

He leaned forward, eyeing me intently. "What exactly is the problem with the simulation?"

I threw my hands up in exasperation. "It just isn't right. It's like painting with mittens on. There's no feel to it, you know?" I gave my seat a shove. My throat felt tight and the words came out high. "I never should have said I could do it. I never should have even bought this ship. It was the dumbest thing I ever did, and we're all going to pay for it." I punctuated the last word with a half-hearted kick to the control panel. After a sigh, I said, "It would be all right if it was just me. I-I'm not really afraid of dying. I just hate the thought of you all having to die with me. I can't stand it." The last ended in a sob.

Pinky was out of his chair, wrapping his arms around me, two to the sides and one patting my head. He was warm and soft and he smelled nice, vaguely spicy. I just bawled. All of the things that had happened to us, all the times hope had been snatched away—I'd just reached my limit. I held onto him like a life preserver, something solid when all the hurt threatened to wash me away. Like I had when I'd broken my arm when I was eight, or when the bullies had gone after me when I'd come back from the last embassy mission, alone. I cried until there was nothing more to cry, and my sobs dwindled to sniffles.

"It just figures, doesn't it?" I pulled away gently, wiping my eyes. "I wanted to honor Mom, to finish her mission. Now I'll go out the way she did, lost among the stars."

"That's not decided yet," he said.

"Sure it isn't."

Pinky let me go and sat back in his chair. He turned his head to face the Window. After a while, he said, "Do you know why I came along?"

I shook my head, wiping away tears. "I don't know...so we'd always have a supply of bad jokes?"

"Hey!"

"Just saying," I said, with a ghost of a smile.

"*Besides* that." He paused. "I came to see the stars."

"Couldn't you have done that on Vatan?"

"It's not the same. On our homeworld we never see the stars. We didn't even know they existed until your people came." He clasped two of his hands together, Pinky's way of showing emphasis. "I moved to Vatan very young, before I could appreciate the stars. Very soon, I learned that I couldn't be satisfied looking at them through any kind of atmosphere. I had to see," he pointed at the Window, "this."

My voice was quiet. "You're not sorry you came?"

"No."

I shook my head slowly. I really didn't deserve Pinky.

"Do you miss your family?" I asked. Mom had been gone for a decade, Dad for longer. Pinky's parents presumably were still around, back on his planet.

He took a few moments before answering. "It's not quite the same," he said, finally. Then he reached forward and gave me a soft rap on the forehead. "Besides, you're my family now. You're my dumb kid sister."

"Hah! Who're you calling dumb?"

"You did first. And hey, if the shoe fits…"

"Pfft. What do you know? You don't even *wear* shoes."

He nodded. "Exactly."

I rapped him right back, softly, above his eye spots. This wasn't the first time he'd deflected when I'd asked about his parents. That was fair. Pinky was entitled to his secrets. I was grateful just to have him as a friend.

"So, what are you going to do?"

"I guess keep practicing. Figure out *Majera's* feel. What else can I do?"

Pinky looked at me, his expression unreadable, as usual. Then he stood up. "Get some sleep, Kitra. Things will be better soon."

He sidled out the door. I sat there for a moment, confused at his abrupt exit. But he was probably right. There was no use butting my head against a duralloy hull. I got up, gave my controls a parting look, and headed for bed.

Launch Plus Twelve (Standard)

There are two ways to make coffee on *Majera*.

One is the old-fashioned, proper way: Fill your metal *cezve* pot with water, enough for one cup. Grind your coffee extra fine, spoon two big teaspoons into the *cezve*, do not add sugar, stir. Apply moderate heat. When froth starts to appear on top, take some and put it in your cup. Repeat as often as you like. Wait patiently seven to ten minutes for the coffee to come to a near boil, but turn off the heat before that happens or the coffee gets too bitter, even for me. Then fill the cups, slowly, so the delicious new head of foam stays on top and doesn't break. Do not add sugar. Let the coffee grounds settle in the cup, drink a glass of water to cleanse your palate, sip and enjoy. *Without* sugar. That's how my family does it, that's how Erkki at *Le Frontière* does it, and that's the way it should be done.

The other way is to tell the Maker to produce a cup of coffee. It takes about 10 seconds. The coffee it makes is…well, it has caffeine in it.

I was on my fourth cup of Maker-made coffee. And my twentieth run through the simulation. The longest I'd lasted was 45 minutes, the fuel gauge up to 24%. As Pinky had predicted, I was getting better, but I still wasn't good enough. There were only 42 hours before we reached the gas giant, and I was going to have to sleep sometime between now and then. Still, what else could I do but practice? I rubbed my bleary eyes, finished the last of the dreadful brew, and punched the panel to start my entry again.

It was over in eight minutes. I pushed the flight sticks away and glared at them.

There was a tap on my shoulder. I yelped with a jerk. It was Fareedh looking, oh, about as bad as I must have looked. There were dark circles under his eyes and his hair was at a stage well beyond cutely ruffled. It was greasy and asymmetrical, like he'd fallen asleep pressed against a wall. For three years.

"Sorry," he said. "I waited until you were done. Have you been at this all night?"

"Yeah."

"Still no good?"

"No."

He smiled then, and it made me furious. Was he laughing at me? I was about to say as much, but he spoke first.

"I have something that might help."

I tugged at my hair, quelling the unreasonable anger. "What is it?"

"Let's try going through the simulation again," he said. His eyes were glittering a bit.

"What good is that going to do?" I asked. "You saw how I did in the last one. I should just get some sleep and try again when I'm fresh."

He gestured to the console, invitingly. "Just once more. I want to see something. You don't have to start from insertion; midstream is fine."

"Sure," I said sharply. "Why not." I settled in, breathed a deep sigh, and lit things up again. Fareedh took his seat behind me. I time-skipped at 5x speed through the first part, the easy bit. As the external pressure hit 100 kilopascals, I dialed it back to normal and tensed for the first crosswind. It wasn't long in coming. The simulated current hit the side of the ship and caused it to yaw around its center. I moved to compensate, very slowly.

And felt my chair press into me as I did so.

I blinked. I pressed gingerly on the stick again and once more felt a slight acceleration. That had never happened before. It *shouldn't* happen. More than that, my subtle corrections weren't having the expected effect on the ship's attitude. We were still being blown off course. So, counter to all the instincts that two days of flying this tugboat had taught me, I pushed hard on the controls, as if I were in a glider.

I was pushed into my seat. *Majera* responded nimbly, straightening out with ease. My eyes widened. An updraft hit the ship, shaking it with turbulence. Not just fluttering the gauges—I felt it in my seat! I pulled back instinctively on the controls, to climb over the simulated air pockets. *Majera* soared up like a hawk, easy as anything. I laughed with delight.

"What's going on?" It was Marta's voice. I turned for a moment, long enough to see her bracing against her chair. "Why is the ship shaking?"

Fareedh was smug. "I made a few modifications to the flight control program," he said.

"You sure did," I said. "This is amazing!" The ship was soaring through the simulated currents, light and responsive for the first time. I wasn't fighting *Majera* anymore. It was like an extension of my body. "What did you do?"

"It was Pinky's idea, actually," he said. "He told me that you wanted the ship to be more like your glider. I set the antigrav to be responsive to your actions to give that feel of motion you were missing. Not too much, but enough to be noticeable. The other thing I added was a translator function, reading your actions at the controls and having them correlate with the ship's position, external factors, and so on." He looked at me hopefully. "Do you like it?"

"Like it? It's wonderful!" I pressed forward on the thrust slider, propelling the ship faster than I'd ever dared push it before. Again, I felt myself pressed into the seat, and *Majera* cut through the simulated clouds steady and true. "You did all this in two nights?"

"Well, I had help."

I felt comfortable enough to look away from the Window, and I saw Peter was there, also looking beat to hell and back.

"Did you have something to do with this?" I asked, smiling tentatively.

"It was his idea to do the antigrav effects," Fareedh said. "I couldn't have done it without him."

Peter nodded in agreement. "Yeah. Well." We made eye contact, and his gaze flickered away. "You needed the help." I felt my smile fade a little. Well, he'd been right. I hadn't been cutting it. And instead of gloating or sulking, he'd helped come up with a solution.

He looked back at me for a moment, eyes hard. Then his expression twitched and softened. "Come on, hero," he said, sitting in his chair. "Let's run this program through its paces and see if we can't hit 100%."

I blinked tears away. I didn't dare bring myself to hope again after being let down and letting everyone else down so many times. But I just couldn't help feeling that maybe, just maybe, our luck had finally turned a corner. I turned to face the Window again, exhaustion forgotten, and hit the thrusters.

Chapter 12

Launch Plus Fourteen (Standard)

Our destination filled a quarter of the bridge's Window, even at no magnification. I curled my lip as I surveyed the sight shining before me.

The third world of this system was not a pretty planet.

I've seen gas giants that took my breath away. Worlds with ring systems like a girdle of diamonds. Planets banded like an old-fashioned Easter Egg, with colors just as vivid. Giants that spin so fast they became tremendous ovals. Even Four back home, though it wasn't so dramatic, at least had the beauty of familiarity as a reassuring light in Vatan's sky.

But not this giant.

The planet was too big, offensively big. Its belts were muted and muddy looking, all blending into each other and making the world look like a huge sandstorm. It had sparse, colorless rings. And its collection of moons was unusually small, with just three round ones and a dozen little rocks. It was like no one wanted to hang around this big ugly monster. Least of all me. I'd come to think of it just as The Giant. And I hoped I was here to slay it. To swoop into it, steal its breath, and escape.

We were an hour from contact, at a point where the course of the ship was still decided by Isaac Newton and Pinky rather than any piloting I could do. If I wanted to (and part of me did want to), I could ask Peter to fire the engines and instead of plunging into The Giant, we'd go into a close orbit. Enough thrust, and we'd leave the giant's gravity well altogether. But then we'd be out of fuel, drifting and doomed. So, of course, I didn't say anything.

I waited on the bridge. There wasn't enough time for another simulation. I was feeling pretty confident, though. If The Giant was anything like what Fareedh had cooked up for me, we had a better than even chance at making it through. I got out of my chair and paced a little circle.

"You nervous?" Pinky asked. He was the only one on the bridge besides me.

I paused, thinking about it. "Not really. More just wanting to get it over with."

He looked at me for a while, not saying anything. Then he turned to face his panel again. "Forty-five minutes to go. We should probably get the rest in here, too."

I nodded, leaned over my panel and punched the all-ship comms. "Time for pre-contact check," I said, hearing my voice echo throughout the ship behind me.

Marta was first in. She gave me a bright reassuring smile that I couldn't help but return. Peter plodded in shortly after and went straight to his controls. After a few seconds of cycling through displays, he nodded. "Ready when you are," he said, his voice neutral, controlled.

"Let's wait for Fareedh," I said, and sat down in my seat. The Giant filled the screen now. Below the Window, several of the virtual gauges had begun to glow a bright orange, their readings flickering at the high end of their scales.

"Peter," I said, pointing to them. "What's going on?"

He answered without turning to face me, his hands and eyes busy with his work. "It's radiation from the planet's magnetic field. We're being hit by the energetic particles trapped in them."

"How long can we fly through this?" I asked.

"*Majera* is pretty well shielded," he said. "A few hours, at least. Just don't go outside."

I chuckled nervously. "Noted," I said.

Fareedh stepped in with a "Sorry I'm late." I noted that he was wearing a black, short-sleeved shirt that I hadn't seen before. When he brushed past me to get to his seat, I smelled the faint tang of sharp sweetness that clung briefly to freshly made clothes. He sat, then turned to face me, a crooked smile on his face. Across his chest, "GO TEAM!" was printed in glowing purple letters. I nodded approval, then broke into a grin. He was such a goof.

"Gang's all here, Cap'n," Pinky said. "Want to call it?"

A deep breath, in through the nose, out the mouth. "Yeah, let's do this," I said, slipping back into my seat and snapping my harness across me. "Time to contact?"

Contact was an arbitrary point, when the atmospheric pressure outside would reach ten pascals—one thousandth of a standard atmosphere—and our wings would have something to bite into. When we'd stop falling and begin flying.

"Thirty-eight minutes," Pinky answered.

"Hull integrity?"

I heard Peter tapping while I looked at the hazy tan swirls filling the screen. "Fine. No breaches in physical or electromagnetic barriers."

"Reactor status?"

"Nominal. Output is clean."

"Reactor core temperature?"

"45 million degrees K," he answered.

And so on down the long checklist. The ship was in good shape, all systems acting like they should. By the time we were done with reports and tests, the first wisps of The Giant's atmosphere, not yet more than a few molecules of hydrogen and helium at a time, were flowing along *Majera's* nose.

"Contact in five minutes," Pinky said.

I flipped the Window for a rear view. It was still black as night. The twin suns, orange and red, were bright disks at the left edge of the screen. I panned the view around until I found Jaiyk, just a fiercely shining dot. I found myself looking at it wistfully. Despite its gloominess and my initial fright, it had had its bright spots, and it was my first (hopefully not last!) adventure. Would we ever go back there? To get more pink stones, if anything. Somehow it didn't seem likely.

A little chime rang, and a popup on the Window showed that external pressure had already hit ten pascals, the density found at about twenty miles above the surface of Vatan. I instinctively grabbed for the controls. They jumped eagerly into my hands.

"Aren't we early for contact?" I asked.

"Sorry, Captain," Pinky said sheepishly. "Planets never behave precisely according to model. You want me to transfer the helm to you?"

I pointed the Window's view forward again, then looked over at Pinky. The ashen light from The Giant gave his rough skin an unhealthy look, and it probably didn't do me any favors either. It felt like the planet was glaring at me, daring me to attack.

"Cut me in."

The flight controls quivered in my grasp, sensitive to the ship's motion. They felt cool and pleasant despite the clammy sweat that slicked my palms. Just the slightest pressure caused a little jostle in my chair, and I heard the others shift slightly, too. Below us was a mottled sea of pale yellow, the tops of the ammonia clouds that shrouded The Giant. I nudged the controls forward experimentally, and *Majera* tipped into a graceful dive. I watched the pressure indicator as it quickly rose to one kilopascal. Thick enough to properly be called "air," but there was still a long way to go before it was thick enough to use for fueling.

The temperature of the hull got dangerously high as the ship scraped against the thickening atmosphere, so I applied negative thrust to slow us down. There was a small jolt as *Majera* passed through one of The Giant's numerous jet streams, wind blowing across our bow at several hundred kilometers per hour. I tensed in anticipation. This had been one of the big stumbling blocks in simulation, tipping us into a spin over and over again.

This time, I kept the ship on its course with barely a bump, no sweat. What a difference the new program made! Fareedh and Peter had truly worked magic. We hit a second channel of invisible rushing air, this one at our tail rather than in front. I compensated with an easy movement in one hand, and we were through in less than a minute. I relaxed into my chair and grinned.

There was no actual moment that the ship reached the upper cloud layer. Instead, beige wisps, puffs of ammonia ice crystals and ammonium hydrosulfide began to stream past the Window with increasing frequency. After a few minutes, I couldn't see the clouds at all – we were in them. I braced myself for turbulence, but there wasn't any so far. The pressure gauge said 18 kilopascals.

That's when we hit the first pressure pockets, invisible regions of higher and lower density air. They bounced me in my seat, and the controls jiggled in my hands as *Majera* was jostled. I strained to make the pockets out in the Window, but I was effectively blind. I couldn't see the air pockets, only feel them when were on them. "I wish I could see better," I muttered, half to myself. "It's like flying through an orange sock."

"Let me switch the view filters," Pinky said. "I'll find us a wavelength that makes things a bit clearer." Pinky's six-fingered right hand played along the panel beneath it, and the view was transformed. Stippled cloud banks curved ahead of us in graceful arcs. Little yellow puffs exploded faintly in front of the ship, clouds of denser gasses ripped apart by the ship's passage. Thanks to Pinky's adjustments, the dangerous pockets showed up as little swirls of trapped, circling air.

"That's perfect," I said. Now I could fly a course through the clear spots and avoid the worst of the bumps. *Majera* stayed perfectly responsive as I dodged left and right on our way further down, as friendly to my touch as my old glider had been.

The pressure gauge continued to climb: 120 kilopascals. 130. The air outside was now almost as thick as it gets on the surface of Vatan, but just as unbreathable as it was on Jaiyk.

And suddenly, we were below the ammonia, the skies completely clear. Beneath us, kilometers away, there was a sea of closely packed cotton balls, and the Window pop-up that monitored chemical composition flipped to completely different numbers and spectra. *Water* clouds! Their whiteness was a beautiful contrast to the dirty yellows of the sulfurous ammonia clouds above us.

I leveled us off about halfway between the cloud layers, the pressure reading 306 kilopascals. This was about as deep as I needed to go. I stopped using the thrusters as brakes, instead angling their output behind us to keep us flying at around Mach 6. We were well within The Giant's troposphere, the dense layer of atmosphere where weather happens, and it took some work to keep *Majera* on course. Still, it was way better than it had been in the simulator before the patch, when just flying in a straight line gave me cramps and sore muscles. I enjoyed the feeling of control, the sensation of simply flying. I just wanted to cruise like this forever. At this altitude, with white clouds arcing gracefully below me, The Giant wasn't so bad. For a moment, I could almost believe I was flying high above Vatan or some other habitable planet. But the endless horizon, with layers of cloud stretching into infinity, shattered the illusion. The Giant was enormous. At our present speed, six times that of sound, we could circle Vatan in less than a day, but it would take a *month* to go around the Giant's equator.

"Are we fueling or what?" Peter's voice, annoyed, broke me out of my reverie.

He was right, I was stalling, afraid to find out what would happen when I opened the fueling ports for real. But our reserves were at 4.6% and dropping. That wasn't even enough left to get us out of the atmosphere. It was now or never. I gritted my teeth and reached for the scoop toggle, paused a moment with my finger over it, then jabbed forward.

Oval panels in the nose slid seamlessly aside, the opened ports breaking the clean aerodynamic lines of the ship a bit. *Majera* bucked as a fraction of the hydrogen flowing over the ship slid inside, where filters could pluck out the heavy hydrogen molecules and discard everything else. When I'd first done this in the simulation, before the boys' patch, the ship had gotten really unstable, tipping over at the slightest provocation. Keeping steady had been like holding a tiger by the tail.

Even with the new programming, it wasn't exactly easy. With the inlets open, *Majera* was a lot touchier. But it wasn't impossible, either. I wasn't wrestling the ship anymore, so it just took a dose of concentration, like any kind of flying.

"Fuel reserves rising!" The relief was clear in Peter's voice. I looked at the panel. Sure enough, we were at 4.8%. A pleasant thrill ran through me, all the way down my spine and out to my toes and fingers. I realized I had been holding my breath. I let it out slowly. I rolled my neck, hearing the joints pop, and felt my lips stretch in a wide smile. Time to show The Giant what I could do.

I started flying in high school. Because I was deathly afraid of heights.

The fear was born when I was eight years old, during a descent onto Sennet, the Provincial capital world. This wasn't my first trip with Mom, but it's the first landing I really remember. A dozen or so members of the Vatan delegation had gathered in the big round observation room of the emissary ship, and someone thought it would be a good idea to blank out the floor for a better view. The announcement was made in French, which I didn't really understand at the time, so I was completely caught by surprise when the ship's deck disappeared. We hung, apparently suspended by nothing, over the spires of Sennet's biggest city. We were *falling*.

I stared wide-eyed at the hover cars that were little shiny ants on the gray highways below. I don't know why I focused on them, but to this day, they stand out vividly in my mind. I screamed and grabbed onto my mother's robe. No matter what she tried, I would not be consoled. I pitched the biggest fit. One of the other passengers offered me a bar of chocolate to quiet me. I took it and crammed the whole thing in my mouth, which muffled my cries a bit, but didn't stop them. Finally, the captain had the good sense to make the floor opaque again.

I didn't go onto the observation deck again for weeks, and never during a landing.

It got worse after Mom died. I found myself avoiding rooftops. I stopped traveling by plane, or even monorail, altogether. When I was twelve, I wrote an essay about how I was going to be a deep sea diver when I grew up, figuring the ocean was about as far away from heights as you could get. I skipped club trips and parties if it looked like I would have to leave the ground to get there. It just became a way of life. Avoid the sky. I missed out on a lot of fun stuff in middle school.

Then I got a letter from Marta inviting me to the spring dance our first year of secondary school.

The prettiest, nicest girl in school had asked me out to the biggest event of the year. I was over the moons, until I found out where it was going to be held: Seventh Heaven, a floating lounge in the swankier part of town. It was one of those antigrav buildings that never land. You have to fly to get there.

My heart seized up just thinking about it. I wasn't going to go, I *couldn't* go. I remember picking up my *sayar*, opening my mouth to call Marta and decline. That's when I realized just how powerful the phobia had become, how much it was messing with my life. I had to face it head on, or it would rule me forever.

There were ten days before the dance. Not a lot of time. I decided to tackle things all at once since I didn't have time to get over my fear gradually. Peter had built up his muscles over the course of a year when he got tired of being terrorized by bullies; I needed to make myself master of the air overnight. So I looked for a flight school. No half measures for me!

I figured there had to be tons of places to learn how to fly around Vatan's capital. I was right, but you're not allowed to pilot a plane until you're sixteen. After some more digging, I learned that, for some reason, you *are* allowed to fly a glider. That was close enough. There was one school close by with openings, and I jumped on the opportunity. Money wasn't really an issue, not with the inheritance, and my uncle was surprisingly encouraging. The only obstacle was fear, and I wasn't going to let that stop me anymore.

I dove right into the deep end; new students were expected to fly on the very first day of training. I was apprehensive during orientation. I bit my nails during pre-flight checkout. I yelped at the first jerk of the glider as its antigrav tug pulled us along the runway and the wheels left the ground. My body was slick with perspiration by the time the tug cut us loose, thousands of feet in the air. I gaped in terror when the instructor behind me released the flight controls and told me it was my turn to fly.

This was it. I held my breath, then took the stick and gripped tightly, like I was hanging on for dear life. At the instructor's direction, I timidly pulled on the controls just a little, back and to the left. I felt the seat press against my back as the graceful craft rose in a lazy arc, a panorama of ocean, city, and river filling the left window. There and then, in the middle of the sky, the fear evaporated as if it had never been, replaced by elation. The glider was doing what *I* wanted it to. We were flying, and *I* was in control. I whooped so loudly the instructor had to cover her ears, but she was smiling, too.

The fear was gone. This was what I'd been born to do.

I was here to slay it. To swoop into it, steal its breath,
and escape.

Chapter 13

"We just hit 60%!" Peter called out, his tenor voice high with excitement. I blinked and refocused myself. I'd gotten lost in my memories.

Majera zoomed far above the puffy white clouds of The Giant, as trusty and obedient a steed as any knight's horse. Its stubby wings wobbled slightly as hydrogen flowed over them at several thousand kilometers per hour. The controls were responsive in my hands, and I held them in an easy grip, adjusting for the occasional shifts in local winds. I couldn't have imagined getting this far just a few days ago.

I wriggled in my seat. I also hadn't expected to be spending so much time sitting down. Pilot's chairs are designed to be comfortable, but I'd been in this one for most of the last hundred hours, off and on, running simulations. My butt needed a break. The pop-ups and gauges showed that things were calm enough for the moment. I unsnapped my harness and then stood up, keeping my hands lightly on the sticks.

"Where are you going?" Fareedh asked, an incredulous tone in his voice.

"Nowhere," I said. "Just sore, that's all."

I heard a little grunt from Pinky. "You don't see *me* taking a break," he chided gently.

"Yeah, well, you don't even *have* a butt," I said.

"I beg your pardon. I do too!" he said with exaggerated indignation, and he started to expand, slowly and deliberately. Like he had at *Le Frontière* when I'd tried to pounce him.

"I take it back!" I said quickly. The last thing we needed was for inside the ship to smell as bad as it must outside. I sat back down in the chair, looked at Pinky, and stuck out my tongue. He responded in kind, a thin extrusion forming below his eyespots. I heard Marta giggle.

The controls jiggled slightly in my hands, and I noted a crosswind had picked up above and to our right. I adjusted our trim and upped our thrust slightly to compensate. The ride got a little rougher as *Majera* hit an unsettled patch of atmosphere. I was grateful for the development. There had been several stretches over the last couple of hours where I'd caught myself falling into a trance staring at the horizon, the two layers of clouds meeting at infinity. It didn't help that I'd been sleep-deprived these last several days.

"You know what'd be great right now?" I said, keeping my eyes on the Window. "A cup of coffee. Real coffee. Does anyone besides me know how to make that?"

"I'd be happy to," Marta said. "I've got the least to do right now."

I turned briefly and gave her a grateful smile. A bump of turbulence made her squeak as she went through the door, and I quickly returned my attention to flying. The air was more unsettled now, maybe because of the crosswinds. I cycled through the filters, trying to find the one that would best warn me of air pockets, but the turbulence remained stubbornly invisible. I'd just have to plow through by feel.

"Can you go back to that last setting?" Pinky asked. I toggled through to the view filter he was talking about.

"What's up?" I hadn't noticed anything.

He raised his middle hand and pointed. "You see that? Clockwise 40 degrees and about 20 up angle?"

I looked where he was indicating. "That little red haze off over there?" I asked.

"Yeah. Let me see if I can get a reading on it." A few taps later, "Ammonium hydrosulfide. It's from the upper cloud layer."

Peter added quickly, "We'll want to avoid it. We can't use that stuff and it might foul our lines."

"Will do," I said. I angled us downward, cutting back the thrust to keep us at a constant speed. *Majera* shuddered as we dove into thicker air. It was a mixed blessing: we'd fuel faster, but the ride would be bumpier.

The smell of brewing coffee hit my nose, making me smile. It also made my stomach growl; it dawned on me that I hadn't eaten in many hours. I had been too nervous to think of food before. Of course, things could have been worse. I could have forgotten to go to the bathroom before we started the run.

I thought about asking for a sandwich, then decided I was thoroughly sick of sandwiches. They had been about all I'd lived on the last several days. We had a lot of bread. That was all I could figure to do with the big bag of flour, and we were saving what was left of the other supplies for the trip home.

I was still wrestling with that dilemma when Marta came back in. She had coffee *and* food, and that was enough to make me seriously reconsider our break-up...just for a moment. I tapped the panel so that it would contour itself to create space for dishes. She put a big mug of coffee into the cup-holder and a plate into the shallow depression I'd made to my left. Steam billowed from the coffee. There were a couple of long beige shapes on the plate, like closed gyros or burritos, but with no obvious seams. No sauce or spices accompanied them.

"What are they?" I asked. I had no clue.

Marta just gave me a smug chuckle. "Try them!" she urged.

I waited a little bit to make sure we were in a fairly steady patch of air. Then I picked up one of the pastries. It was warm and dry to the touch. I nibbled at it tentatively, without much enthusiasm. I was certain it was more bread.

It was absolutely *delicious*. Past the crumbly coating, my tongue encountered a burst of flavors. Savory, meaty, creamy. "Good Lord, Marta! How did you make Wiener schnitzel hot pockets? I thought we were out of beef."

"It's actually a chicken-fried steak recipe," she said, her voice dripping with pride. "And we are."

"Then how...?" My voice was muffled. I'd crammed a third of the pocket in my mouth, it was so good.

"I told you I could do more with flour than loaves of bread," she said.

My eyebrows shot up as I looked at her. "This is *flour*?"

Marta had the satisfied look of someone who'd just executed a checkmate or caused a cluster-wide revolt in *Empires*. "I took the gluten protein out and made steaks of it. With the right spices and a little milk, voila: chicken-fried protein pockets. Perfect for eating and flying at the same time."

"You're a genius, Marta," I said with absolute sincerity.

"Is there one in there for me?" Peter kept his voice casual, but I thought I heard a little hurt in his tone. I quickly reached for the other pocket to offer it to him. Marta rapped my hand gently with her fingers.

"Don't be silly," Marta said. "I made some for everyone." She flashed Peter a warm smile. He returned it, looking a little sheepish. Marta ducked through the door again, on her way to the galley.

I hadn't realized how hungry I was. I finished the first pocket with one more gulp and took an experimental sip of the coffee. Nice and hot. I drained it quickly and grabbed the second pocket, opening my mouth to take a wide bite. Then my seat lurched against me, and the food flew out of my grasp. I grabbed the controls with both hands as *Majera* bucked up and down like we were rolling along a corrugated sheet. I pulled up to get out of the layer of disturbed air and the starboard wing caught a crosswind, rolling us to our left. I didn't fight it. One direction was as good as any for now. I let the gust dictate our course, like a breeze on a wind vane. We stabilized, and I looked for my lost pocket. It was a sad heap on the floor.

"Marta should have let me give it to you after all," I said to Peter.

"I'd just have dropped it, too."

I heard Marta come back in. "What was that?"

"The outside air is at 400 kilopascals," Pinky answered for me. "It's soupy stuff."

"It's good, though," Peter said. "Our fuel is up to 70%. Less than an hour and we're set."

Marta made little tsking noises and picked up the dropped pocket. Then she ducked out again, probably putting it back in the Maker so its components wouldn't go to waste. I frowned as I looked out the Window. "Guys, does it look like there's more of those red clouds out there?"

The little puffs had become ribbons of maroon, like thin curved highways in the sky. Most of them were above the ship, but a few spiraled down far in front of us. Where they approached the water cloud level below, white clouds stretched upward to meet them.

"It looks like a large-scale weather pattern up ahead," Fareedh said. "Some kind of cyclonic storm? It's destabilizing the cloud decks."

"What happens if we fly through it?" I asked, an edge to my voice.

"It depends how established the cyclone is," Fareedh answered. "Winds will be higher, for sure, and if it's a full storm, they'll blow strong at right angles to the center. We'd want to ride with the current. If the cyclone is still forming, the winds will be slower but more chaotic."

"Why don't we avoid the storm altogether?" Peter asked. "Can't we go around it?"

Pinky made a strange chuffing sound. "It could be bigger than you think. It goes between both cloud layers." He was silent for a moment, considering the tendrils of ribbony red corkscrewing in the Window. "It's probably as big around as Vatan," he said at last.

That floored me just thinking about it. How could I have missed something so huge? But then, a world-sized storm was just a tiny pockmark on The Giant, and like the thermals back home on Vatan, this one had been largely invisible.

"Maybe we should go back the way we came." Marta had returned.

I nodded, eyeing the red ribbons. "Sounds like a good idea." We weren't going anywhere in particular after we were done fueling. We just needed to get far enough away from The Giant to jump. I eased *Majera* into a starboard bank. At the speed we were going and with the thickness of the air, it would be a wide turn, but that was fine. There was plenty of time before we'd reach the red ribbons ahead of us. I settled back in my seat as the ship began its stately curve.

Something pummeled the ship with a hammer blow, sending us into a downward spiral. Only my hard grip on the sticks kept me from falling out of my chair. I'd forgotten to snap my harness after my butt break! I heard a thump and an 'oof' from Fareedh, informing me his harness was unfastened, too.

"What the hell was that?!" I called out, desperately turning *Majera* into the tumble to try to regain control.

"Wind," Pinky answered. "Going...wow... six hundred kilometers per hour." He was gripping his chair with two arms and tightening his harness with another. "The cyclone must extend further out than we thought," he continued. "This is one of the outer arms."

I managed to get *Majera* partially stabilized.. We were now corkscrewing downward, heading right toward the spinning plain of thunderheads below us, but the ship was responding to my control again.

"We're at 600 kilopascals," Pinky said. "We need to pull up."

"Easier said than done," I shot back. I couldn't just yank the sticks toward me to put us in a climb. That'd be fighting the current and I'd lose control again. I bit my lip and tried to feel my way around the winds. They were curling mostly down, a little to the left. All right. We needed to go back the way we came and get altitude. I couldn't turn, and I couldn't climb. That left one option.

"Everybody make sure you're strapped in tight," I said, pulling my harness into position, dismayed at the poor example I'd set. I waited a moment. "Everyone ready?" I called. There was a chorus of answers in the positive.

"I'm not going to like this, am I?" Marta squeaked.

"Nope," I admitted. I made one last visual estimate of the distance to the lower cloud deck. There should be just enough room.

I rolled the ship upside down.

Inverting the *Majera* wouldn't have made a difference if our antigrav had been on normally. We wouldn't even have noticed except for the horizon turning over. But because of Fareedh and Peter's modifications, things basically responded to force and gravity as they'd behave on a plane without artificial gravity. I heard a clatter as unsecured items fell onto the ceiling throughout the ship. I felt my ponytail pointing straight up. Then I pulled back on the sticks, pitching *Majera* into a steep, inverted dive.

"Are you crazy?!" Peter shouted.

"Probably!" was all I could manage. The dive got steeper and steeper, until we were fully vertical, our nose pointed straight at the water clouds. Already, our view was getting blurry with the haze off the cloud deck. I couldn't feel the wind currents tugging on us anymore. We must have driven right through them. I yanked on the controls again. Our speed was tremendous, and I had to get us out of the dive before we went too deep. *Majera* was slow to respond, but little by little the nose of the ship creeped up. At last, we were flying level again, the ship's bow spearing little puffs of water clouds as we zoomed along in the exact opposite direction to when we'd rolled to begin the Split S maneuver. I pulled back once more, upped the throttle, and this time, no blast of wind kept us down. We soared into a climb.

I heard a whoop of joy and was surprised to find it wasn't me, but Fareedh. "That was amazing, Kitra!"

"For Infinity's sake," Peter said weakly. "That could have killed us."

"Nah. She knew what she was doing," Pinky said. He lowered his voice to a stage whisper. "Right?"

I answered at the same level. "I'm still not sure I know what I'm doing." Then I called out, "Can I get a status report?"

"Uh," Peter fumbled, "Air pressure is 630 kilopascals and dropping. Fuel reserves are at 78%. We need at least 12% more to be sure we can make a Jump back to Vatan."

"That doesn't sound bad."

"Yeah, but intake contaminant levels are rising. We can't keep fueling like this for long or we'll blow our lines."

"The hurricane must be pulling in all the junk from the clouds, even if we can't see it," Fareedh said.

The ship shuddered again, a massive tail wind pushing at *Majera's* aft. We weren't out of the woods by any stretch of the imagination. The atmosphere around the ship roiled like water in a coffee pot, transmitting every disturbance to us, thanks to Fareedh's antigrav modifications. A small price to pay—I couldn't fly *Majera* without them. I caught a flicker of amber light out of the corner of my eye and saw it came from the fuel system indicator on The Tree. I risked a glance at the internal diagnostic diagram and saw that temperatures were too high in the fuel lines. Gas was streaming into our pipes so fast that our systems were overheating. The filters were working harder from all of the contaminants, which wasn't helping the situation.

Another jerk of the sticks, and I got us into a fairly smooth channel, moving with the winds instead of tacking through them. The fuel tank indicator read 82%. I throttled back, trying to give our tired fuel system a rest.

"Pinky, can you do something to make the sulfur and ammonia show up better?" I asked.

When he didn't answer, I started to call his name again. He waggled his left-most hand shushingly at me. I knew that gesture: Pinky was feeling overwhelmed and needed me to stop talking. He found the filter he wanted, and the cream colored vista in the Window transformed into a salmon-tinted haze, overlaid with burgundy patches. One patch was dead ahead. I pulled up, and we climbed over the worst of it. That put another red puffball in our path, and I dodged to the left to miss it.

Thanks to all this crazy flying, my stomach had developed an odd hollow feeling, and I felt sweat prick on my forehead. Now I was glad to have lost that second gluten pocket. Behind me, I heard murmurs of thanks from Fareedh and Peter. Then, a hand appeared over the panel, palm up. It was Marta's, and inside was a little blue capsule. Anti-nausea. Leave it to Marta to think of everything, and to take care of everyone. I took the pill from her, but considered for a moment just toughing the ride out. Then we hit another bump. I popped the medicine in my mouth and swallowed.

The stuff worked fast. My stomach settled back into quiet mode, and none too soon. From the wind-speed warning pop-ups and the fast moving clouds, it was clear that the hurricane was still raging around us. We must have cruised deep into it without knowing because, even heading straight away from its center at high speed, it showed no signs of abating. I examined the Window and tried to work out the most efficient way around the contaminant clouds Pinky had made visible for me, at the same time guessing which way the winds would be blowing.

It was too much, too fast. Red puffs streamed to either side, and then the mother of them all came up at me like a fist. I banked hard, then rolled nearly sideways to cut between two crimson twins. That bought just a moment's respite; the view in front of me was so peppered with red, it was like a 3D minefield. My eyes were watering with the strain. There had to be a way out.

There! A clear patch down and to the right looked like it offered clear cruising for a ways. I banked toward the new course and was almost immediately rewarded by The Tree's fuel system warning light flickering back to green.

"86%!" Peter said, hope tingeing his voice.

"You sure that's not enough?" I asked, flexing my fingers one hand at a time.

"We won't want less than 90%," Peter repeated. "And we'll need enough fuel to get out of this gravity well, too. You'll want to fill us to max before we leave."

"That's my plan," I said, gritting my teeth. *Just a little more.* If I could maintain this balance of pure hydrogen and high density, we'd be topped off in no time.

The smooth patch continued, and flying became less demanding again. I was able to actually think, to concentrate on something beyond the next turn. We were almost done with the run! My thoughts turned to the immediate future. We'd fill up with fuel and then what? Pinky would plot a fuel-efficient course out of The Giant to some safe distance. I'd gently climb us out of the atmosphere. Once we got out far enough, we'd hit the Drive.

And a week later, we'd be home.

Home! Since our accidental Jump, this was the first time it seemed within reach. I made a promise to myself: nothing but in-system flights for a long time after this.

The Tree blinked at me, snapping me from my private thoughts. Yellow on the fuel system again. The temperature inside our collection chambers was climbing rapidly. I looked at the Window, confused. There were red clouds above and below us, but the path immediately ahead was clear.

"What's going on?" I called out.

Again, Pinky waved his hand at me, his eyespots intent on his panel. Then he toggled through filters, the Window taking on different tints and textures. After four or five, our view blanked out entirely, obscured by white water vapor. "Lord!" I exclaimed. "We're in the middle of a cloud bank."

Klaxons sounded as The Tree went red, first in the fuel system, and then in several subsystems. "There's water vapor clogging up the fuel lines," Peter shouted. "Line temperature has spiked above safety limits. I've got to close the intakes."

I checked our status. "We're only at 94%. It's not enough."

"It's that or burn out the fuel lines, Kitra! Or the engines!"

Our ship was literally drowning in flight. If we lost the engines, we were done for. "Crap. All right, do it."

Majera shimmied slightly as the vents closed, changing the aerodynamics of the wings again. The Tree remained stubbornly red.

"Why isn't it helping?" I asked.

"See for yourself." Peter popped up a sub-window on the screen to show me what he was looking at. There were red patches all along the wings of the ship. "Something must have melted," he said. "The fuel scoop system is offline. We're overheating. We've gotta get out of this atmosphere. The friction is going to melt us."

"How am I supposed to get us out of the atmosphere without going *through* the atmosphere? And the faster I go, the more friction there will be."

"You've got to do something," Marta said, sounding afraid.

Something. But what? Reducing speed would put us at the mercy of the winds, and a gentle climb would keep us in the soup too long. No, there was just one way out: I had to put us in a vertical climb to get out of the atmosphere as quickly as possible. That'd use a lot of fuel, though.

Well, one problem at a time.

"Hold on," I shouted. Then I pulled back on the controls with a jerk. When *Majera* was standing on its rear, I pushed the thrust to maximum.

The force crushed me into my seat. My vision grew dark, the gees forcing blood into the back of my brain. The displays said *Majera* was pushing 10 gees of thrust, way more than the ship could handle long term, and it didn't feel like much less for me. I cursed Fareedh's patch. It didn't feel like the antigravity was working at all!

There was a vague smell of something burning, but I couldn't tell if it came from the cabin or inside me. I tried to call up the external air pressure gauge, but my vision grew too blurry. I gave up and devoted my energies on keeping us on course, straight up out of the thick air. Alarm bells sang in jarring harmony. We cleared the ammonia cloud level, and the sky became a uniform dark brown. The red light on The Tree showing the fuel line status went ominously grey. At least, I thought it did. It was so hard to see, or do, anything.

The acceleration abruptly vanished, the crushing weight leaving me in a rush. Panic rose in me, tasting like vomit. We were still deep in The Giant. If the engines had gone out, we'd fall back and be crushed. I looked at The Tree. It was dotted with red lights. Yet the engine indicators were all green. Our thrusters were still going steady.

"I turned off the compensation program," I heard Fareedh say. "There's no reason for it anymore, and I thought I heard something crash in the galley."

"Good thinking," I rasped. We were climbing fast. The air gauges already read below 10 kilopascals and thinning fast. Stars began to shine in the darkening sky. It looked like we were going to make it.

"Peter, how are we doing?" I asked.

"Fuel scoop system's offline. We're not going to be able to fuel again without a base. But..." He trailed off, and I looked over at him. He was busy cycling through displays. "Internal temperatures are dropping rapidly. I don't think anything else failed."

The air outside was under 500 pascals now and dropping quickly. Another minute of thrust, and we were essentially in vacuum again, though far from free, yet, of the Giant's gravity.

"I'll go see what fell down," Marta said, unstrapping herself. I looked up at the Window to make sure we weren't heading into the plane of the rings or the moons. We weren't, so as long as the ship stayed together, we should have no trouble getting to Jump distance.

"Oh no!" I heard Marta exclaim.

"What's wrong?" I croaked, my throat dry. I knew it. Some critical piece of equipment must have gotten mangled in the climb.

"I'm sorry, Kitra. One of your cups broke."

I let out a bark of a laugh. "Worse things could have happened."

I relaxed back into the chair, the utter lack of feedback in the sticks and chair so odd after the long, turbulent flight. I exhaled in a rush, completely drained but exultant. I glanced idly at the gauges, pausing at the fuel pop-up.

Oh no.

I looked away, then at it again, but the numbers were the same. We were at 88%.

Not quite enough to get home, and with no way to refuel.

Chapter 14

The radiation counters rose and fell as we passed through The Giant's vast belts of charged particles. I angled *Majera* so we were heading over the planet rather than out, building enough velocity for a safe orbit. Then I turned off the engines and took one last look at the fuel gauge. 86%. Plenty for anything we wanted to do.

Except go home.

Numbly, I gave the helm back to Pinky. I fought back tears, staring unseeing out at the stars. I felt utterly used up, rudderless. I couldn't just sit there, though. So, somehow, I found the energy to stand. They all looked at me, Fareedh's expression calm, Marta's hopeful. The tendons of Peter's temple moved in and out as he clenched his teeth. I tried to make my face a mask, to hide my disappointment. We'd gone through so much, making it so far, just to be stopped so close to our goal. I couldn't break down in front of them. I had to remain strong.

"Well, we're not quite out of the woods yet," I said, attempting a light tone. "Why don't we take twenty minutes to recharge, and then let's meet in the wardroom and see what our options are."

Peter opened his mouth, then shook his head and walked out without a word. Fareedh blinked a couple of times, as if he was having trouble processing what I'd said. Then he gave me a weak smile paired with a sloppy salute, and left.

"You going to be okay?" Marta asked. Her eyes were searching mine.

I waved her concern away. "Yeah, of course. I just want us to have our heads clear. It was a long flight."

She frowned, unconvinced. Then she turned, went through the door, and it was just me and Pinky. He hadn't gotten up, nor did it look like he intended to. "I'll see you in twenty," he said.

"You're not taking a break?"

"No. I need to think." He turned away from me and sat in silence. I felt rebuffed.

I was too tired to dwell on it, and the coffee Marta had given me had worked its way through and wanted out. I went to my room, took care of business, and flopped out on the bed. I stared at the ceiling, then closed my eyes, the gentle glow from the lighting panels leaving after-images behind my eyelids. My brain was utterly blank, stretched beyond thinking.

My *sayar* began to chirp. Before I could pick up, the call was forced open from the other side. "Kitra? Are you coming? It's been half an hour. We're all here." It was Fareedh's voice. I must have fallen asleep.

I blinked my eyes and inhaled deeply. "Yeah," I said groggily. "Be right there."

I stood up, started to topple, and had to grab the display table to stay upright. Gravity seemed at odd angles to the floor. I steadied myself and stepped toward the door. It felt like I was walking on pillows.

It was a little better once I got inside the wardroom. I stole a quick look at the counter; there was a cup missing from my mom's set. I felt a vague emptiness as I sat down.

"So… any ideas?" I asked. I certainly didn't have any.

The others looked at each other, waiting for someone to take the lead. Finally, Pinky leaned forward and said, "I don't have any, as such. But I can restate the problem as I understand it, and maybe that'll shake something loose for someone else."

"Go for it." My voice was practically a croak.

He waved a hand over his *sayar*, and the familiar 3D starmap appeared over the table, this time with the twin star system of Anya/Atya at its center.

"We're here, in the middle," he said, "and this is the maximum range that we can Jump." A purplish overlay extended out in a sphere from our position. "Vatan is over there." One of the stars at the edge of the map, just inside the purple zone, turned bright green.

"But…it looks like we can go all the way to Vatan," I said, confused.

"It looks like it," Pinky echoed, "but fuel use in Jump is somewhat variable." He made a chopping motion with his middle hand, and the outer layer of the purple sphere turned orange. "There's the margin of error. Vatan's right in the middle."

"Plus," Fareedh added, "we're going to use fuel just getting out of this planet's gravity well so we can Jump."

"Yeah," Pinky said. The sphere shrunk slightly. Was Vatan outside of it now? I squinted up at it. Yes, no matter how I looked at it, Vatan was out of range. We couldn't Jump straight home.

"What about these other stars?" Marta asked, pointing at the few dots that lay in the desert between us and Vatan. "Couldn't we use these as stepping stones?"

I looked at Peter. He didn't answer. Instead, Fareedh clicked his tongue against his teeth. "Those systems aren't settled. Nowhere to get fuel or supplies."

It was so hard to think. "We're so close," I managed to say. "Maybe we could Jump as near to Vatan as possible and send out a distress call."

"A distress call that goes at the speed of light," Pinky said. "No one would get it in time. And it would still take them a week to get to us. Longer if they traveled in normal space."

Marta spoke up, "What if we lighten the ship? Could we increase our range that way?"

I looked wearily at Pinky. He was silent for a while, his shoulders rippling oddly. Then he shook his pseudo-head in a very human gesture. "No, it wouldn't work. We couldn't strip enough of the ship away to make much difference. Even Peter's conglomeration of spare parts doesn't amount to enough."

Peter coughed, or snorted, or something. Maybe it was a laugh. I looked at him again and saw he was just staring at the table, this little smirk on his face, beaming out *I told you so*. A rush of anger filled me, momentarily cutting through the exhaustion.

"Well, Peter? What have you got?"

He didn't look at me. He just focused on the table with flat eyes, the maddening smile still on his face. Finally, I stood up and snapped. "For crying out loud, Peter! The rest of us are trying to figure out how to get out of this mess. Are you going to help or just sit there and gloat?" I barely got the words out. Standing up suddenly must have caused all my blood to fall to my feet. A wave of vertigo hit me, like I was falling down a deep shaft. My stomach lurched and my vision grew blurry. The room spun wildly, the ceiling panels far too bright.

Peter looked up at me and blinked. Then his eyes widened with concern, and his lips parted. I never heard what he planned to say, though, because the floor rushed at me and I blanked out.

Smell came back first: the plastic and metal of electronic components, a faint mustiness, the tang of old sweat. Slowly, the rest of my brain came online. There was a conversation in hushed tones, too low for me to make out, underneath which a gentle, rhythmic pinging played. Softness pressed from beneath me, some kind of bed. A sour taste made itself known in my mouth, and my throat was raw, sore.

I didn't want to open my eyes. I wanted to just go back to where I'd come from, that nice emptiness from worry or danger. That damned pinging kept playing on a nerve, though. First I had to find its source and turn it off.

My eyelids parted then quickly shut. It was too bright. I tried opening just one partway. That was tolerable. The ceiling swam into view, not the dappled faux sky of the wardroom or the familiar pattern of my stateroom. Where was I?

"She's awake!" a high voice cried, loud enough to make me wince.

"Hey, Kitra," someone else rumbled. "We were worried about you."

I blinked and looked as far to the left as I could manage without moving my head; I wasn't ready for that yet. There was a stack of shelves up to the ceiling with boxes on them. Where had I seen them before? Rolling my eyes to the right, there was a little table with a *sayar* on it. It pinged to itself and displays hovering above it showed numbers and squiggles. Like a hospital diagnostic. I was in a hospital?

Marta walked into my field of view. She wore a wide smile but her eyes narrowed in concern. Her brown curls fell loose and untended. "Welcome back," she said. Her voice caught at the end, and she swallowed.

"Back?" It came out as a rasp, so I coughed and repeated the word. I turned my head toward her and was rewarded with a stab of pain behind my forehead. But now I recognized where I was: the workshop. This section had been cleared out and turned into a makeshift infirmary.

"Am I sick?" I asked.

"That's what I thought at first," Marta said, "but aside from a low fever, I can't find any evidence for a bug." She looked levelly at me. "Just how many cups of coffee did you have over the last few days?"

"All of them?" I answered, feeling a tiny smile playing on my lips.

"And no sleep, yeah?" Fareedh walked into view. He made a funny contrast to Marta, all angles versus her curves.

"I had a few hours," I said, tilting my head back to look at the ceiling.

"Mhmm," Marta said. "I think exhaustion, plus those gees we pulled getting out of the gas giant, did a number on you. You haven't eaten enough either, and what you did eat..."

"...I had to clean up off the wardroom floor." Peter's face appeared over mine. "Hey, hero," he said with a crooked grin.

"Hey, mouse. Sorry about the mess."

"S'fine. We're just glad you're okay."

Memories of the meeting came back to me. We didn't have enough fuel or a way to get more. We weren't okay at all. And Peter had just been sitting there like a lump. I'd gotten up to yell at him. A ghost of the anger I'd felt tried to well up again, but exhaustion dulled it to vague irritation.

"I do have good news," Peter said, a little tentatively. "I think I figured it out."

I rolled onto my elbow, then winced as my head tried to explode. I gritted my teeth until the pain subsided. "You what?" I managed.

"What Pinky said triggered it," Peter said, looking over his shoulder, perhaps at Pinky. "As soon as he said it, I realized we could do it." He looked back at me and chuckled, "My junk pile. That's the answer."

I looked at him blankly.

"I'm talking about the capacitors for the beam weapons that used to be installed," he said.

"What does that mean for us?"

He pulled up a chair and sat across from me. "We need a certain amount of power to go into and out of Jump. We don't have quite enough fuel to generate the power for Jump to Vatan." His eyes glowed. "But the capacitors could make up the difference."

I looked at him incredulously. "You can do that?"

"Sure. Juice is juice."

"And you just, what, plug them in?"

"It's a little more work than that, but essentially, yeah."

I tried to process what he was telling me. It made sense, but I'd never heard of anyone doing this before. I wondered why it wasn't standard practice on ships to have a backup battery. Maybe it was; it's not like my experience was super extensive. One thing nagged at my mind, though, something that would keep the plan from working. I struggled for a second before it came to me, my brain still feeling fried.

"Don't we have to charge them?" I asked. If we had to use fuel to energize the capacitors, then they wouldn't be any help. Power was a zero-sum game.

Peter's eyebrows rose. "Oh no. I did that before we left Vatan. They're fully charged." He smiled again. "It's best to be prepared."

I snorted, just a little. That's what he'd said last time we were in this room together. So there was a way home after all. I tried to get excited about it but all I felt was lousy. He hadn't been ignoring me in the wardroom; he'd been making a plan to get us home. And I'd yelled at him for it.

"What can I do?" I asked. My voice caught.

"You?" Peter asked, his voice gentle, eyes shining. "You've done enough, Kitra. More than enough. It's my turn now." He put his hand on mine. "You sleep. Sleep for a week if you want. I've got this."

I looked at his big fingers over mine. It still amazed me that he could do such delicate feats of engineering with those.

"That's fantastic," I sighed, rolling onto my back and closing my eyes.

And I was out like a light again.

"I hate to ask, but are you sure this will work?"

Chapter 15

Launch Plus Sixteen (Standard)

I slept all of the next day and much of the one after that. Sure, I woke up now and then to go to the bathroom, and once to wolf down a bowl of soup someone had left for me, but each time I couldn't wait to hit the sack again. It wasn't until the third morning that I opened my eyes and felt caught up. My mind was clear, and my worries seemed manageable again. I could think in straight lines.

My first stop was my stateroom for a quick wash and change of clothes. I went to the wardroom afterwards and flipped through the options on the Maker. Marta's schnitzel pockets were on the list now, so I printed one of those, blew on it to cool it down, and ate it in four bites. I was just swallowing the last of it when Pinky padded in from the bridge.

"How're you feeling?" he asked, resting easily on a tripod of legs.

"Like myself again." I even sounded human. "You?"

"Oh, pretty good shape. Subject to change, of course." He turned his spherical body into a cube for a moment by way of demonstration. An old joke, but I smiled anyway. It was good to see him. "Peter's gotten a lot done," he said. "Have you seen it?"

I shook my head, licking crumbs off my fingertips. "I just got up. And after what I said to him the last time we were in here...I'm a little embarrassed."

He jerked a big thumb aft. "Go check it out. It's impressive."

I brushed off my hands and made to go out the back door. Pinky stopped me with a big hug from behind, pseudo-arms curled all around my middle. He rested his head on my shoulder. "I'm glad you're okay. You scared me. All of us"

I turned around to embrace him properly, squeezing him tight. "I'll try not to do it again."

Pinky let me go and reached up to give me a pat on the head. "Okay," he said. "Now you can leave." He turned and walked back toward the bridge. I smiled fondly at him, watching the two grooves along his middle where I'd hugged him slowly fill up again as he headed out of the room. Then I went aft.

Peter's contraption was in the very back of the ship, in the service corridor under the Drive. This hall was normally kept empty; that's how it had been when we first inspected the ship at auction, and aside from cleaning the dust out and re-covering the floors with gray carpet foam, we hadn't done much with the space. Now it was filled with a pile of components and tubing that, honestly, didn't look much different from when they'd been a bunch of separate pieces of equipment in the cargo bay. It was obviously a kluge, looking more like something out of the 19th century instead of the 29th. In the middle of it all was Peter, squatting over where the mess plugged into the wall.

"I hate to ask, but are you sure this will work?" I immediately regretted the words. I should have started with an apology.

Peter stood to face me, wiped his high forehead and put his hands on his hips. "Yes. It's basic physics. The hard part was just coming up with a housing for the capacitors." He pointed to the big cylinders that sat in the middle of the contraption. I didn't want to think about how many gigawatts of power had been sitting in those batteries the whole flight. Navy ships used them to power ion guns that would rip ships apart at a range of 100,000 kilometers. What if they'd blown up while we were shaking around inside The Giant?

Well, it was a moot point. If they could get us home, that's all that mattered.

"Is there any way to test it?" I asked.

"Sure," he said, and pointed to the wall where cables fed from his kluge to jury-rigged sockets. "I'm wiring it as a fall-back to the power supply battery system. It'll show up on our screens as extra energy."

"I mean, how will we know it works under live conditions?" I asked.

"Ah." His grin was lopsided. "We Jump."

I snorted. "That's reassuring."

"It'll work," he said. "Honestly, that's not what you need to worry about." His tone was still light, but his expression had darkened some.

"Oh?"

"You saw Pinky's map," he said. "Vatan's still at the end of our range, and fuel use isn't perfectly predictable. Pinky and I have done the math the best we can, but..."

I frowned. "You're saying we still might not make it all the way home."

"We should. There's a lot of juice in those batteries."

"But we might not."

He nodded. "Yeah. We might not."

I bit my lip. Then, "What happens if we don't have enough fuel for that?"

He shrugged. "Ships that get lost in Jump don't make reports."

A beat passed. "Do the others know?"

"Yeah," he said. "I told them while you were sleeping. They're all right."

I reflected on that, watching the contraption blink and hum quietly to itself. I licked my lips and said, at last, "Hey. I'm sorry for yelling at you the other day. I don't know what got into me."

He smiled ruefully. "I don't blame you. I've been kind of a jerk."

"Oh no," I said, shaking my head.

"It's true." He looked earnestly at me. "I've spent most of the last two weeks sulking, waiting for *Majera* to fall apart, for us to die."

I didn't know what to say.

"I'm a coward," he went on. "Always have been. You know that. Space scares me, hyperspace really scares me." He lowered his voice. "Losing Marta scares me." I looked away at that. "No, it's not your fault," he added quickly. "It's mine. You worked so hard to keep us going, when we had no clue what to do. You found the refinery on Jaiyk. You flew us through that gas giant and got us the fuel we needed to go home. Me? I've had my head up my ass."

He pointed at the contraption. "I hope this makes up for it. To both of you."

I stepped forward and wrapped him in a hug, blinking away tears. "Thank you for everything you've done, Peter. I know it's been hard. You must have been scared to death."

I felt him shake his head. "No. I've decided I'm not going to be scared anymore. Whatever happens will happen. If we don't make it, at least I'll be with friends." He pressed me away gently and put his hands on my shoulders. "But I'll tell you this, if we make it back," he said in almost a whisper, his voice quavering just the slightest bit, "the school had *better* give me credit for this project."

I choked on a laugh, then decided to let it out. He joined me with a quick chuckle. It was clear Peter was putting on a brave face, but that was way more than I could ever have expected from him. Maybe more than I deserved.

"I'll make sure of it," I promised.

Launch Plus Seventeen (Standard)

Peter and Fareedh told me their kluge was fully hooked up and ready to go early the next day. I called us all to our stations right after. With our food and air supplies so limited, the sooner we left, the better.

The Window was split into three vertical panels. The middle was the real-time view, currently displaying the new constellations I was starting to get used to. The Giant was behind us now, thankfully out of sight. The left side of the Window was taken up by the local star chart. Pinky's sphere now showed three colors at its edge: a new red shell extrapolated the extended range our capacitors gave us. Vatan lay in that shell. On the right, directly over Pinky, was our in-system navigation map.

"We're ten radii away from the gas giant," the alien said. "Minimum safe Jump distance."

"How're we looking otherwise?" I asked.

Peter spoke up, "Fuel is at 85%."

"Air recycling system at 88% efficiency," Marta said, a note of chagrin in her voice. "Not what it could be, but it should last a week with our current reserves."

I eyed the navigation chart. "Let's drift a bit," I said. "Might as well risk as few safety margins as we can."

"Aye, aye, Cap'n," Pinky said. "I'll make the numbers work for when you give the order."

The order. All I had to do was say, "Let's go." My voice caught in my throat, and I coughed instead. What was holding me back?

I glanced over at The Tree for reassurance. All of its symbols glowed a cheery green with the exception of the refueling subsystems, which were grayed out, thanks to our trip through The Giant. There was a little pop-up showing our battery charge. It used the standard icon, a long and cylindrical container with a little bump on the end filled with blue to indicate charge level. I never knew what that icon was supposed to represent; it certainly didn't look like any battery I'd ever seen. The pop-up read 436%, and not only was the blue spurting out the top in a big spray of liquid, but there were little animated figures in swimsuits playing in the shower. I smiled. Fareedh's doing, I was sure.

If I still had the capacity to smile, things couldn't be too bad. I took a deep breath and exhaled, decision made

"We're probably far enough out now," I said. "Peter? Want to do the honors?"

I looked over at him. He nodded with a tight smile. Then his eyes widened, and he exclaimed, "Almost forgot!" He reached for the bottle of anti-nausea capsules on his panel. He popped a couple in his mouth and swallowed. "Anyone else want some?"

"I think I'm good," Fareedh said. "I'm ready for it now."

"Tough guy," Peter said. "Marta?"

"Sure," she said, taking two from him.

"Pinky?" Peter held the bottle out.

"No drugs for me," the alien said. "I'm a fan of clean living."

Peter rolled his eyes but if he had a choice comeback, he kept it to himself. "On your command, Kitra," he said. I noted he didn't offer me any capsules, which was kind of flattering.

"On my mark," I said, then swallowed. "Three. Two. One. Mark."

This time, we were all watching the Window as we made the transition into Jump. A hole appeared in the sky, a circle of darkness quite different from the blackness of space. The stars seemed to crawl away from that hole, slowly at first, then racing. It wasn't really the stars that were moving — we were flinging ourselves into that hole, an all-consuming nothing that lay in a direction the human mind couldn't imagine. I was ready this time and shut off the screen before Jump space filled it. The cramps hit right after, doubling me over, even braced as I was for them. I wished I'd taken a pill after all.

"We're in Jump," Peter announced, a little raggedly.

"I noticed." I was still catching my breath. "That was a rough transition. Are you sure everything's all right?"

Peter didn't answer for a while, checking over his panel. Finally, he said, "All systems report within tolerance." He turned to look at me. "It's the oversized battery," he explained. "It punched us through to Jump space hard."

"Not too hard, I hope," Fareedh said.

"I...I don't think so. Well, it doesn't matter anyway. We won't be doing that again on this flight." Peter pointed at the battery pop-up. The little people had disappeared, and the icon was empty.

"What's our fuel at?" Marta wanted to know.

"46%" Pinky replied.

I swiveled the chair to look straight at Peter. "Is that enough?"

He tried to smile, but his eyes remained solemn.

"I don't know," he said.

Chapter 16

Launch Plus Twenty (Standard)

The next several days were a drag, just like the first time we Jumped.

Before the trip, I'd had the idea that the seven standard days in Jump would be the best part. Other than ship maintenance, there were no responsibilities, no worries. Nothing happens in Jump, but nothing can happen *to* you. I figured it'd be a non-stop party with tons of good food, fun holos, and long games. Sure, I was in the piloting business for the exploration, but that was no reason getting there couldn't be half the fun.

There's nothing like the feeling of impending doom to kill a good mood. We tried to keep our spirits up, but Peter's words were always in the backs of our minds. The fact was, no one knew what was waiting for us at the end of the week. Whether we'd have enough fuel to get out. What effect the harsh catapult into Jump would have on our exit. We only knew that we might not have much time left.

I was brooding on this grim line of thought as I entered the wardroom for breakfast the third morning after going into Jump. No one was there yet. The table was bare, and most of the shelves were retracted. It was funny. Before the flight, we'd had all of these plans to decorate the ship with custom posters, murals, souvenirs, stuff like that.

The room wasn't entirely empty. Sprawled across the port wall on the lone shelf that was out was a set of four smudged transparent containers with little dark boxes attached to their sides. They hadn't been there yesterday. I walked over for a closer look.

Each one was about a half-meter wide, a little less than that in depth, all filled with moist dirt. Terrariums of some kind, I guessed, though there weren't any animals in them. A greenish-gray film covered the soil in the containers. The black boxes affixed to the containers each had their own little *sayar* screen. From the numbers and graphs on them, I deduced that they were environmental regulators, keeping the air make-up, pressure, and humidity at certain levels. I realized a moment later they were set to Jaiyk's levels. The green stuff was the same sludge I'd found on the beach.

I whistled low. Marta had *really* gotten a lot out of my little sample!

I heard footsteps behind me and knew it was Marta without even looking. We all had our own preferred footwear that made distinctive sounds against the floor. Peter wore slippers; Fareedh had his sandals; me, my work boots. Pinky didn't wear anything, of course. But Marta usually wore low heels, even shipboard.

"Aren't they great?" she said, coming up beside me.

"The containers?"

"Yes, the samples. They're doing nicely."

I shrugged. "If you say so. Looks like sludge to me."

She gave my left shoulder a gentle punch. "That's because you're not a biologist. I've isolated three different species so far."

I looked over the containers. "I still don't see why you needed to set them up in here."

"Well," she said, tapping at the screen on one of the Jaiykariums. "My room is full, and I wanted them some place I go often so I wouldn't forget to check up on them." Then she chirped, "Ooo!"

I looked over at her. Her curly hair was swept back behind her head leaving a couple of locks framing her round face, and she had on a purple sundress with a subtle gold pattern to it. She was pointing to the aft-most box. It seemed more smudged than the others. I stepped up to it and saw that threadlike tendrils of the stuff had crept halfway up the sides.

"I'm playing with different temperatures and wavelengths of light," she explained. "Looks like I found a winner, at least for this species."

"Um, are you sure this stuff isn't going get out and take over the ship?" I asked, only half-kidding.

Marta wrinkled her nose. "No, silly. If it got out, it'd die. The oxygen would kill it."

"Well, that's a relief." I eyed the stuff warily, then shrugged. Marta knew biology.

It was quiet, the ship's air circulators and the gentle hum of the specimen box environmental controls a soft background noise. I became conscious of Marta's body heat, radiating close by. I casually took a step away, sideways.

"Kitra," Marta said, her tone serious. "Is something wrong?"

I turned to face her. "Uh... what makes you think that?" I asked.

"This is the first time we've talked to each other alone in two weeks." There was a little crease between her big green eyes.

I realized I had started rubbing the fingertips of my right hand together, and gripped the nearby chair to stop. "It's just been busy, you know?"

"If it's about," she hesitated, "what I said before, I'm sorry about that."

"No, it's fine." I looked down at the floor.

"Things are a lot better now with Peter. Thanks to you."

I looked up. "Me?" I asked.

"Yes, you." She smiled gently at me.

"What'd *I* do?"

Marta paused, sorting her thoughts, then said, "Do you remember when we went hiking the Goldayi trail?"

"Sure, right before we met Fareedh. We got lost. Our tent got rained out. Pinky got that terrible rash from the local berries."

"Which you told him not to eat."

"Yep," I said. "I sure did."

She smiled, then said, "Peter told me afterwards the trip was the best thing he'd ever done."

I snorted. "Really? We almost didn't make it back."

She nodded. "But we *did* make it back. You made sure of that, always keeping us going. You pushed him out of his comfort zone, made him do something he never would have tried on his own." Marta took a step toward me and put a hand on my shoulder. "He thinks the world of you, Kitra. We all do."

I blushed, speechless. What could I say to that?

She looked down at me and sniffed slightly. "We're still best friends, right?" Her eyes were pleading.

"Oh, Marta," I said shaking my head. "Of course." We fell into a hug, and I closed my eyes, resting my head on her shoulder with a happy sigh. "I missed you too," I said. I hadn't realized how much.

"Oooh. Can I join the party?" I jerked around, startled. Pinky was in the doorway to his room.

"You...!"

"Blob?" he offered.

I rolled my eyes. "No. Jerk." I said. "Scared me half to death."

"That was not my intention," he said. He made a show of bowing. He doesn't exactly have a waist, so he creased in the middle and bent low. He was in a symmetrical form, about a meter-and-a-half tall, with two thin legs and four spindly arms. When he straightened out, I saw that two of his arms were filled with rough-surfaced beige balls, maybe 10 centimeters across.

"One moment, please," he said, placing his load onto the table in a pyramid. Then he stepped back into his room. Marta and I looked at each other. She shrugged, as clueless as me.

Pinky came back with another pile that was bigger than the last. He set it down in a heap next to the other one, but he kept one of the balls and tossed it casually from his inner left hand to his inner right. "It occurs to me," he said, eyespots following the ball back and forth, "that we, as a crew, have been in something of a slump."

"Ye-es?" I said, getting worried.

"I have taken it upon myself, as the most balanced and well-rounded crewbeing, to remedy this situation." He cupped his second left hand, his fingers fusing together, and raised it to just below his eyespots. It was purely a dramatic gesture; Pinky's voice comes from his whole body, not just where a mouth would be on a human. Then he hollered in an uncanny imitation of my voice, "Peter! Fareedh! Hurry - something's wrong!"

I heard a thump from behind the door to the Shop. The door opened and Peter appeared, his expression worried and his fingers grimy. He must have been working on a project.

"What's going on?" he asked, then stepped aside as Fareedh squeezed in beside him, just in time for Pinky to bean Fareedh with the ball. It hit him on the left shoulder, making a squishy noise and leaving a light residue on his starburst-patterned t-shirt before falling to the floor with a faint splat. Fareedh looked at the alien as if he was crazy.

"I hereby declare this to be a Day of Rest," Pinky intoned in a low, commanding voice. "Work is canceled on account of snow." Then he picked up another ball, turned around, and smacked me right on the forehead.

I should have ducked. Pinky's not that fast. I was just so flabbergasted by the attack that I couldn't move. I bent down and picked up the ball, now a little flat on the bottom. It wasn't made of snow, or even cold at all. It was flour dough moistened and packed into a rough sphere. I straightened up and glared at Pinky with a wicked smile curling my lips. He just looked back at me calmly and reached behind him with two arms to pick up another pair of balls.

"FOOD FIGHT!" Fareedh yelled, and he let loose with the doughy projectile Pinky had hit him with. Let loose at *me*, the fiend! I ducked under it and threw mine at him. It bounced off the wall harmlessly.

"Oh crap," Peter yelped, and he darted for the table, gathering up an armful of balls. I grabbed the one Fareedh had thrown, made like I was going to return his attack, and instead bopped Pinky on his...well, on his center of mass, anyway.

Chaos broke out. There must have been six balls in the air at once. I scooped a few off the table and crouched behind a chair. Marta cried out, "Watch out for my specimens!" and raced to raise a barrier on her shelf, attracting a hail of missiles in the process. That just gave her ammunition. She whirled around and smacked Peter and me in rapid succession. Marta was *deadly* accurate.

"Isn't it a bad idea to waste all of this food?" I asked, the words coming out ragged between giggles. I punctuated the last with a line drive to Pinky's pseudo-noggin.

"We'll just throw them all back in the Maker," Marta said with a laugh, her arms windmilling another pair. These hit Fareedh in his bony little butt as he was trying to gather more doughballs. Marta and I looked at each other, nodded, and ducked behind a couple of chairs with full armfuls of ammo.

"Boys against girls?" Fareedh said with mild disdain. "How quaint."

His next shot bounced off of Marta's chair.

Pinky stepped back until he was against the front wall. "I refuse to take sides in such a fight," he said, and then flung a shot at Fareedh followed by one at me.

I don't know how long we went on like this. Pinky must have made thirty of his faux snowballs, and they held together pretty well. There's only so many times you can splat one against a wall or a face, though. Over time, the balls lost their integrity, bursting upon impact rather than bouncing off, leaving us covered head to toe with little beige impact stains. As the fight went on, I was spending more time scrounging for ammo than throwing it. One of the last intact dough-balls burst in my hair, followed by an evil cackle from Marta.

Some ally she was! I looked around frantically for a ball so I could return fire. Were there any left? There! One solitary doughball, under the table. I saw Fareedh on the other side and knew he'd spotted it at the same time. We both ducked and lurched forward for it…and crashed our noggins together. I sat back and rubbed the top of my head, and he did the same, though he was still grinning. The ball was useless, squished. That pretty much ended the game.

We emerged from under the table just in time to see Peter sail in through the door to the shop. He flung a ball that must have flown out of the wardroom earlier. This final projectile poofed into dust right in the center of Pinky's face.

The alien didn't bother to wipe the dough from his face and body; it just slowly disappeared into him while he calmly waited for us to stop panting and giggling like crazy people. Finally, in a dignified voice he said, "That went off rather well." His normally pink skin was a deeply amused brown.

"Hey," Marta said cheerfully. "After we tidy up, who's in for a marathon game of *Empires*?"

I looked at the layer of crumbs that covered the floor. It was going to take some doing to get it all back into the Maker. Well, even if we lost a little, we'd saved our other provisions for this week anyway. Food wasn't going to be an issue.

Turned out morale wasn't, either.

"Count me in!" I said.

Launch Plus Twenty Four (Standard)

I chuckled for days over our "snow day," though it was a while be-
fore my head stopped being tender from my run-in with Fareedh's.
Pinky's free for all snapped the cord of tension that had run through
the ship, allowing us to actually enjoy ourselves the next three days.
But harsh reality lay around the corner. Once the time remaining until
Jump-out dropped below 24 hours, things started getting tense again.
The last twelve hours, we kept largely to ourselves. Not unhappily or
awkwardly. More like in contemplation, making our peace.

For the first time in years, I prayed. Nothing formal, just a plea
for safe passage. I wasn't even sure who I was praying to. Certainly
not the Lord that Mom prayed to five times a day and in services on
the Sabbath. He was never very real for me. Just a convenient place to
lodge requests or a name to invoke for emphasis. No, I was appealing to the Universe as a whole, the harsh, unfeeling set of quarks and
space-time that was all I believed there was. I knew it probably didn't
care about me, at least the way Peter and Marta believed. But it was
worth a shot. It made me feel better, anyway.

An hour before Jump-out, we made our way to the bridge and ran
through the checkout lists. Conditions were 'nominal;' the ship was
reasonably healthy. There was nothing to do but wait.

And nothing in the universe moves slower than a watched clock.

Every time I glanced back at it, about half as much time had
passed as I thought should have. It got so bad, I started to wonder
if it was some quirk of hyperspace. After an eternity, the Window
pop-up chronometer finally reached ten minutes and zero seconds.
It seemed to hang there, frozen. Then it continued downward. In less
than ten minutes *Majera* would leave Jump. Or we'd find out what
happens when there's insufficient fuel to leave Jump. I tapped my
fingertip against my knee, continuing to watch the ship's clock tick
away. Pinky placed a pseudopod on my hand. The spongy warmth
was a comfort, as was the calming scent of cinnamon he exuded.

What would it be like to fail a Jump-out? I wondered. Would we
just stay suspended in hyperspace forever, while we slowly starved
or suffocated? Would subjective time slow to a crawl such that stars
would spawn and die in the time it took us to take a breath? Or would

the ship get crushed at the barrier to normal space, spreading its atoms across the length of the universe?

Even if we made it out, there was the chance that we'd end up in the wrong place, somehow. That'd be just as bad; we had no time to spare. There was already a strong earthy overtone to the air, and it felt a bit more humid than normal. Not quite as alarming, but still not pleasant was the other odor, underlying everything: even though we had been as conscientious about hygiene as we could be given the rationed water, body smell builds up. I tapped at my panel. All the atmospheric percentages were still within tolerances, but I had my doubts that the system would last us another week, Marta's efforts notwithstanding.

For that matter, I didn't think *we* would last another week. Doughball fights and *Empires* aside (Peter won this time), we were at the end of our tethers, mentally. There's only so long that you can be on edge before something snaps.

I sat up in my seat, trying to remember how many times we'd evaded death after the blind and accidental Jump. Fareedh finding the trap in our old software. The safe landing on Jaiyk when we were out of gas. Finding fuel at the refinery. Marta's bag of flour. Fareedh's piloting software patch. Surviving the refueling in The Giant. Oh, and when the ocean on Jaiyk tried to eat me and Fareedh. Getting safely into Jump using Peter's kluge had been number eight, and number nine would be getting out.

Nine lives. That sounded right. I just hoped the counter reset after every trip.

I stretched in the chair, eyes still on the clock. "So, what are you going to do when we get home, Pinky?" I asked, a little too lightly.

He was mostly ball at the moment. He overflowed his seat at the sides, two big arms and three little ones thrusting out from his chest. His eyespots revolved around his pseudo-head to face me. "I'm going to find the hottest, stinkiest steambath," he said, "and I'm going to sit in it until I turn inside out. How about you?"

It took me a moment to process that mental image. What *was* Pinky on the inside? Custard?

I said at last, "I'm going to turn my Captain's Log into something I can sell. A book, maybe. Use the money to restock the ship right, and then go out again." I hadn't even formally decided on the plan. It just popped out of my mouth. "That is, if you guys still want to ship out with me."

Pinky nodded his head at me without hesitation, but Peter said, "As you say, Kitra: one thing at a time." The familiar tightness in his voice was back.

"That's fair," I said. He had only promised me one flight, after all. The thought made me sad, though.

"Five minutes," Pinky announced. I resisted the urge to check the clock again.

"Let's start running exit checks," I said.

"Ship's *sayar* reports nominal function, all components," Fareedh said in a brisk voice. Then, more casually, "Peter, how's the transition going?"

"No spikes or unexpected fluxes," he said. "Fuel consumption remains nominal. We're at 38%, for now."

Pinky typed at his panel, and a real-time projection of the Yeni Izmir system—home—expanded in front of the Window. The *Majera*'s expected Jump-out position was a blinking dot. "I've got a course standing by for home," he said. "Navigation controls are still locked."

"Hey, what are the chances we'll Jump-out on top of another ship?" Marta said, sounding a bit worried.

Pinky swiveled eyespots backwards to face her. "Very low, but not zero," he said. "This isn't a scheduled flight. There could be traffic in the area."

"Can you adjust where we come out so it's not in the normal pattern?" I asked.

"Yes," he said, turning his eyespots forward and typing again. "Consider it taken into account."

The ship's clock showed less than 60 seconds to Jump-out. The numbers counted down, green and luminous.

"Energy to Drive increasing," Peter cut in. "Usage still as expected."

His words were punctuated by the tingling in my hands and feet that signaled a return to normal space. My inner ear fluttered.

"Here we go again," Marta said uneasily.

My eyes were glued to the chronometer. Just like before, I caught my lips moving, mouthing the seconds to Jump-out. I shook my head and took one last look around the bridge, maybe my last look at anything. Peter's eyes were locked onto his screen where a schematic of the engine glowed in neon orange. Marta was chewing her lip, absorbed in her own thoughts. I turned my chair. Fareedh was looking right back at me, smiling. Then he winked. I stared at him a second, feeling my cheeks warm. Then I scoffed and swiveled frontwards again. Pinky, I saw, had braced himself against his panel, as usual.

"Fuel down to 5%!" Peter called out.

Crap. I was suddenly certain it wouldn't be enough. I closed my eyes as Pinky recited the final countdown.

"Four. Three. Two. One."

My stomach roiled, and the ship seemed to shudder without actually moving. I waited, resisting the urge to check our status. We were safe as long as I kept my eyes closed, I thought.

"Kitra!" Marta's cry was laced with relief.

I blinked my eyes open, my vision momentarily a blur. The Window was alive, but what did it show? Awful nothingness? Something new? I wiped tears away. Stars! The Window was crowded with stars!

I clutched at the controls, my ears tuned for the sound of a collision klaxon. Nothing.

The Jump nausea receded. We were alive in normal space! I grabbed at the flight sticks, but they were loose and unresponsive.

"Control to me," I said, my throat tight with emotion.

"It won't do you any good," Peter said. "Fuel is at 0%. We're on emergency batteries."

I swallowed. "Where are we?" I asked, knowing that any answer but one would mean we were out of luck.

In response, Pinky angled the Window around. The crescent disk of a planet swung into view, unmistakable with its rings, green skies, and light-dotted continents on the night side. Its day side shone fiercely bright against the star-speckled background.

Vatan. We'd made it.

I whooped at the top of my lungs, and it wasn't just me. Then we were all out of our harnesses, exchanging hugs.

The ship's radio crackled to life. "Ship registration number GF456L," a voice called out. "You are outside the normal traffic pattern. Do you require assistance?"

"I'll say," Fareedh laughed.

"What do I tell them, boss?" Marta said, looking down at me from within our group embrace.

"Tell them we're going to need a tow," I said through a grin. I hoped insurance would cover it.

"Aye, aye," she said, disentangling herself and taking up her post.

Home. By the skin of our teeth, home.

Chapter 17

Twenty fourth of Wind, 308 P.S.V. (Launch Plus Thirty (Standard))

Compared to the big new park they built over the site of the original starport, the park in the heart of Denizli's Old Town isn't much: just a crescent-shaped stretch of green with a couple of long walking paths. But it's still my favorite park in the city, beautiful, and bypassed by tourist hordes.

I sat on a bench in a clearing, still marveling at the freshness of the air, the lack of duralloy walls. The trees around were dense, giving the impression that I was in the middle of a forest, though I could hear the hover traffic just beyond, out of sight. It was all very familiar, solid. The three weeks we'd spent lost in space had a dreamlike quality. Had we really been to the edge of the Frontier and back? Had we really come that close to being lost in space? Whenever I thought about it, I got overwhelmed.

I heard footsteps, turned, and saw Fareedh coming down the winding path. His sandals made little scraping noises as he walked. He'd clearly gotten some sun; he was back to his normal dark coloration after having faded a few shades shipboard.

"You're early," I called out, waving.

"That's true," he said. "I decided to beat the crowd." He sauntered up and gestured to the bench. "Mind if I join you?"

I shook my head, and he sat down next to me, folding his legs underneath him to sit cross-legged. I'd noticed that it was his preferred sitting style when he didn't have to strap into a chair.

"So…" I began. "How've you been? I've hardly seen you since we got back."

"The family flipped out when I told them about the trip," he said with a pained look. "Mom cried for days. Dad said I was irresponsible." He quirked his lips. "My sister thought it was pretty cool, though."

"Sorry about putting you through that," I said.

He waved his hand dismissively. "It's fine. They're going to have to get used to it. Next time might be worse."

"Next time?" I looked at him, hopeful.

"Of course." His eyes flashed with excitement as he looked at me. "When are we going out again?"

"I wasn't sure if you'd want to. It was a close call."

He leaned his thin body back against the bench, stretching an arm along its back. "Sure was."

"We almost died."

He nodded. "Couple'a times."

I smiled. "That doesn't bother you?"

"Of course it does. But you got us out of it just fine, and man, what a ride!"

"You had a pretty big part in us making it, too," I corrected him.

"That's definitely true," he said smugly. Then his smile softened. "You had the hard job, though."

I shook my head. But I didn't actually deny it. I *had* done some pretty awesome things.

"How about you? How are you doing?" he asked.

"Honestly? I can't wait to go out again." I wrapped my arms around myself, hands on my shoulders. "I feel all cramped up."

He laughed. "You were in a ship for three weeks, and you feel cramped out here?"

"Absolutely." I stood up, paced a couple of steps. "You know, when I was a kid, I saw a new world every month. I took it for granted. Being stuck on one world for a decade...I hadn't realized how much I wanted something more until I got it."

"You sure got 'something more' on this trip," he said.

"Yeah. It was tough at the time, I know that. But, now that we're safe, I realize I enjoyed the hell out of it, even the hard parts. I got to see a system I never would have gone to otherwise. I freakin' dove into a giant planet. *We made it back!*" I said, triumphantly.

He nodded, his eyes glowing. "Exactly."

I smiled, breathing in deep and exhaling. "You get it."

"Yep."

"Okay then." I sat back down and leaned against the bench, staring out at the trees. There was the gentle roar of traffic. A breeze picked up, snatched and whirled some falling leaves, then died down.

"Oh," Fareedh said suddenly, digging into his pockets for a moment. "I've got something for you."

I looked at him. "What is it?"

He held out something pink between his thumb and forefinger. It sparkled.

"From the beach!" I exclaimed. He nodded and handed it to me.

"For your collection," he said.

"I lost mine..." I said, softly.

"I know."

I looked down at the stone. It was as beautiful as I remembered. More so under the brighter light of Vatan's golden sun, the swirls inside dancing as I turned it over in my hand. Now I had a souvenir from Jaiyk. I felt a floaty feeling in my stomach, and an urge to jump for joy. I looked up at Fareedh, lips framing a "thank you."

He had sprouted two big pink bunny ears behind his wavy dark hair. Behind them, I saw a familiar pair of eyespots in an otherwise featureless pink head.

I snorted.

"What?" Fareedh asked. I motioned for him to turn around. He did and let out a startled, "Gah!"

"Good morning," Pinky said. He folded his two arms, including the overlong fingers of his left hand, behind his back and rested easily on three thick legs. "Sorry I'm late."

"No problem," I said. Fareedh looked back at me and I put on a mock serious expression that lasted half a moment before my smile broke through again. It had been pretty funny.

"It's just us? Peter and Marta aren't here yet?" Pinky asked.

I shook my head, then dug out my *sayar* to check the time. It was 15 minutes past when we were supposed to meet. There were no messages from them, either.

Pinky walked over to the bench opposite ours and sat. "How's

Majera?"

"Ship-shape, except for the hydrogen scoop lines," I answered. "The tow bill came in. Insurance paid most of it."

"That's good," he said. "Will they pay to repair the ship?"

"No," I said with a frown. "It's okay, though. We're not in a hurry to fix the fueling system, so long as we stay in-system." I smiled at Fareedh. "No more random Jumps for a while."

"I can live with that," he said.

"I wonder what kind of paying gigs we can get," I mused.

"We'll have to get licensed and bonded," Fareedh observed. "It costs to do that." He rubbed his stubbly cheek. "Chicken and the egg, right? How do we make money if we need to spend money to do it?"

"I've got a little left, even after towing," I said. "Enough. I'm not worried. Not about that, anyway."

I looked down the paths, then at my *sayar*. Peter and Marta were half an hour late now. "You think they're not coming?" Fareedh asked.

"I don't know. What do you think, Pinky?" I tried not to sound worried. It wasn't like them at all to be late.

Pinky shrugged. "I haven't talked to Peter in days. The last thing he said to me was something about my smell." He made a sniffing sound. "*He* should talk."

"Did he smell?" Fareedh asked. "I didn't notice."

"I've got a lot more nose than you," Pinky replied matter-of-factly.

The sound of footsteps reached us, and we all looked toward the source. But it wasn't them. Just a jogger making her way through the park. She goggled at Pinky's weird form for a moment before shifting her gaze to straight ahead. A few seconds later she'd disappeared among the trees.

I sighed, got up again, and started to pace. If Peter had decided he'd had enough, then that put us in a serious bind, especially since that meant Marta probably wouldn't be coming back either. That would leave us with no engineer, no one with medical skills, no one to tend the life support systems. Worse than that, I'd be without two of my best friends.

"What do we do if they don't come?" I asked.

Pinky waggled thick fingers at me. "Don't borrow trouble."

"I'm just asking."

"We could double up on jobs," Fareedh ventured calmly, both arms on the bench back now. "Stay on safe runs. Keep away from adventure until we find more crew."

"That could work," I said without enthusiasm. I looked down at the dirty path and scuffed my boot against it.

A moment later, I heard footsteps again. "Hey guys," I heard Marta call out. I looked up and saw her hurrying up the path, skirt billowing around her as she ran. She had Peter in tow, holding his hand. When they reached us, I saw Peter was scowling. My heart sank. I knew he was going to say no. Could I blame him?

Fareedh waved casually from the bench, not getting up. "Kitra was worried you weren't coming."

"I was not," I said unconvincingly, looking down at the ground again.

"I thought you messaged her," I heard Marta say.

"I did! I recorded it right after the train broke down."

I looked up. He had pulled out his *sayar* and was inspecting it. His frown softened. "Oh. It would have been nice if I'd hit transmit."

"Whoops," Pinky said cheerfully.

Hope made me giddy. "You mean, you're not bailing on us?"

Peter looked surprised. "Huh? No way." A smile brightened his face. "Kitra, I wanted to tell you. The data set I got from the two Jumps was terrific. I spent all week reducing and analyzing them. That thing we did with the capacitors gave some weird results, and I'm going to write a paper about it. My professor said I could take the next few months to work on it for full credit." He beamed at me. "I can write it on the ship as well as anywhere else."

I looked over at Marta. "You in, too?"

She nodded. "Of course. All my plants are there. I don't want to have to move them again," she said with a giggle. "Besides, we never got to go shopping."

I felt a warmth flooding my chest, and my lips quirked up on their own.

Pinky made a throat-clearing sound . "Well," he said. "Now that that's all settled." He looked at me and reached behind him with his right arm. "I Made something for you back on the ship, but I never had the right opportunity to present it."

He withdrew something floppy and white from…well, I wasn't sure where Pinky had been hiding it. It was probably better that way. He handed it to me ceremoniously with two hands. It was a flattened circular bag with a hole in one side and a black visor sticking out of it.

I raised an eyebrow. "A hat?" I wasn't quite sure.

Pinky nodded. "A captain's hat. I printed it from some old patterns. They used to wear these in the wet Navies." He placed his hands on his middle. "As I've said, hats are very important."

"Try it on!" Marta urged.

The hat was light and felt strange on my head. "How does it look?" I asked.

Peter mirrored his *sayar* and held it out to me so I could see myself. It looked absolutely ridiculous, something like a flattened version of Pinky's chef's hat, but with a big star insignia in the center above a black visor. It didn't really go with my outfit or anything else I might wear. I loved it.

I looked at my friends, one to the next, feeling my eyes mist up. Fareedh uncurled his legs and stood, facing me.

"Now you look the part," he said. Then, with a smile and a sloppy salute, he added, "Captain."

About the Series

Back when my father was a kid, they had science fiction books for young adults and kids. They called them "juveniles", and they usually featured a young hero flying to the stars. I grew up on these and loved them.

Over the years, YA became all about dystopia and fantasy. I enjoyed The Hunger Games and Harry Potter as much as everyone else, but I missed the space adventures. I wanted to see stories that weren't zero-sum game fights against a Big Bad, that featured reasonably accurate science and characters who struggled with realistic problems. Tales of friendship, ingenuity, and wonder.

That's why this book exists. I hope you like Kitra's first adventure. There will be more.

~

The lifeblood of every author is audience feedback. Please consider leaving a review (of whatever length) on Amazon, GoodReads, or your favorite platform.

About the Publisher

Founded in 2019 by Galactic Journey's Gideon Marcus, **Journey Press** publishes the best science fiction, current and classic, with an emphasis on the unusual and the diverse. We also partner with other small presses to offer exciting titles we know you'll like!

Also available from Journey Press:

Sirena by Gideon Marcus - Book 2 in the Kitra Saga

One starship, six friends, 10,000 lives in the balance.
    Young captain-for-hire Kitra Yilmaz has gotten her first contract: escort the mysterious Princess of Atlántida beyond the Frontier and find her a new world. It's a risky job, fraught with the threat of pirates, dangerous squatters, and rising romantic tensions.

I Want the Stars by Tom Purdom - A Timeless Classic

Fleeing a utopian Earth, searching for meaning, Jenorden and his friends take to the stars to save a helpless race from merciless telepathic aliens.
    Hugo Finalist Tom Purdom's *I Want the Stars* is one of the first science fiction novels to star a person of color protagonist.

Sibyl Sue Blue by Rosel George Brown - The *Original* Woman Space Detective

She is: Sibyl Sue Blue, single mom, undercover detective, and damn good at her job. **She wants:** to solve the benzale murders, prevent teenage deaths, and maybe find her long-lost husband. **She will:** seduce a millionaire, catch a ride on his spaceship, and crack the case.

DO YOU WANT TO
TRAVEL BACK
IN TIME?

WWW.GALACTICJOURNEY.ORG

CPSIA information can be obtained
at www.ICGtesting.com
Printed in the USA
LVHW090234050222
710188LV00001B/69